First publish
ISBN: 978-0

Published by:
The Wacky Wordshop.
40 Emmerson Way
Hadleigh
Suffolk
IP7 6DJ

http://thewackywordshop.co.uk

To Sue
from Laurie

10/10/13

Sweets on the Lampshade

Laurie McPhun

LAND OF NO CLOUDS

Like a butterscotch cheesecake rising from a blueberry sea with floating candle-trees glimmering through a clementine haze, Auransantia embraced the clover-green fishing boat as it sailed into Fesachoni Bay. Columns of sugar-coated stone rose from the waterfront, leaning lazily against listless hills too beautiful for the threatening absurdity of civilisation. They could have passed for living creatures rather than inanimate objects awaiting destruction in a vicious sea.

§

A trio of gnarled, bronzed bodies occupied the boat. A middle-aged couple, with near-identical short brown hair, wearing garish carton shorts and drinking from the same bottle of tasteless but expensive 'huddlers wine' stood 'engine side'. A huge wad of luggage separated them. The woman was taking far more time over her sustenance than the man; his eyes were fixedon the boat's shabbily dressed, seemingly ageless captain. He, in turn, was prodding at a trawler net full of invisible fish while admiring the woman's bare, liver-spotted arms.

"I'm really going brown Dave ... imagine how we're going to look in a few month's time?" she said.

"It's how we're going to feel in a few month's time that I'm worried about. I mean, I know we've been here sixteen times and always thought of it as a kind of paradise, but how much, truthfully, do we actually know about the place?" replied the husband.

She stared at him, confused, like a wealthy victim of a masked assailant, then her face regained its image of contented glee surfing on sapphire-tinged waves of limitless opportunity. She was a spirited girl.

"But, darling, you've only got to remember what the Thomsons used to say a few years ago. Kevin was madder about Auransantia after living there than he'd ever been before; head-over-heels. It was as much as

Melinda could do to drag him back home for a couple of nights at Christmas. He needed a bottle of vodka before every flight!"
"Yeah, well, poor old Kev ..."
"Lovely, lovely man, God rest his soul."
"The worst thing was, he never got to explore the tilting golf course on Prasanollar island. That was always his dream and you can hardly accuse Kev of being 'just a dreamer'".
"And his death; the awful timing. And poor Melinda, being so far away from all her friends after it happened."
"Are you saying there's a good time to die?" asked Dave.
"That's not what I mean and you know it, but for something like that to happen when she was at her most vulnerable ..."
"Of course. Though, er ... we can't really be sure that he actually is dead."
"What?"
"Well, there was no sign of a body, or anything resembling one in the area after he went missing."
"Yes, but aren't you forgetting ... the broken remains of the speedboat he'd been spotted in earlier that day; all of his burnt clothes washed up on the beach, and the barman at Dorillja's ... he'd served him no less than five shots of Tinkabell vodka before breakfast?"
"Maybe, maybe. All I'm saying is, not everyone in a camping shop makes tents." Dave shrugged.
"You're certainly holding out more hope than Melinda ... apparently she's already packed most of his belongings off to England."
"Oh, I wouldn't say she's given up. The thing with the clothes and stuff is, I reckon, simply a gesture to block out her sense of helplessness, a way of regaining a tiny bit of control."
"It's a very expensive gesture," muttered the wife.
"Do you honestly imagine she's thinking about money right now?"
"No one can ignore financial considerations, can

they?"
"Kevin never did. What was it he used to say when their lodger went down with winter flu?"
"I can't remember."
'The cash machine's broken down again' ... "I think that was it." The woman let out a mean chuckle, and left a trace of lipstick on her husband's mottled grey chin.
"We've arrived ... Monsieur, Madame," said their captain.

§

General Malverzeign paced confidently across the balcony. Crowds had gathered in the cobbled courtyard below, like vampires around an open wound. He was proud of his people. He approved of their brightly coloured clothing, grateful smiles and unrelenting cheerfulness. No hardship would be too great for them to endure and no guest would ever be welcomed as anything but a superior.
"Is my blazer ready yet, do you think?" asked the General. His secretary, Elvizina Collonium responded, "Not long now, Sir. Mary's just tying on the yellow ribbons." Elvizina was a tall man. He had red, unhealthy looking eyes, a curved beakish nose, heavy eyebrows, and charcoal coloured hair flopped around his ear on one side, rising to a spectacular ridge on the other.
"Perhaps you should address the nation while I wait?"
"What would I say?" asked Elvizina in his awkward, sometimes French accent. He wasn't thrilled at the invitation. His last public speaking engagement, a year earlier, had ended in disaster when a drunken heckler had rushed the stage. Orders, nevertheless, were orders and there seemed little to gain from arguing with a man who was a personal friend of every gun runner in the South Pacific.
"Don't be long now, Collonium, you know that our glorious public are guardians of a very particular temperament." Nodding to his leader and mentor

Elvizina strolled through the french windows above St. Heramiaouw's entrance hall and shuffled nervously onto the balcony. His heart rate soared. His ears sang. He leaned on the fragile-looking, elegantly carved, horse-shaped turrets and raised his arms in a feeble attempt to signify power. The crowd laughed. "MALVERZEIGN! MALVERZEIGN! MALVERZEIGN!" they roared. He was trying to compose a sentence in his head. A humorous response? Nothing. Within seconds the general had regained centre stage and begun serenading the masses with short, rasping bursts of verbal wisdom. Elvizina was reduced to 'prop' status. With a carefully rehearsed air of spontaneous melodrama he sank to the floor, as though in awe of his master, and cried. A mechanically generated gust of wind swept across the courtyard causing hats to flutter about like feathers while long, neatly braided hair was left to waft greedily over wondrous eyes and handsomely chiselled cheekbones.

"Lords, ladies, boys, girls, soldiers, sailors, farmers, flailers, boxers, bakers, undertakers, let there be no doubt! Our victory is magnificent! A triumph not only for ourselves but for the generations of peoples on this island who will never again have to face the wrath and tyranny of foreign rule. Achieved against all odds, by virtue of our spirit and passion which would never have existed but for the fierce knowledge that overcomes all physical limitations! It recognises no boundary but the universal and invisible principle so familiar to, yet so debased by, a million shamed empires fading into the blackened emptiness of human history!"

§

"D'you think they sell top-up cards?" asked the woman. She was following her husband into the sunlit chaos of a convenience store.

"I shouldn't think so," replied Dave. He was leafing through a three day old copy of the DAILY FEAR,

Britain's second most popular daily newspaper. MOTORWAY MADNESS: WHY CARELESS DRIVING IS DESTROYING OUR SOCIETY screamed the front page headline, concealing a huge advert for Negarkka people carriers on the next sheet. Dave ignored both features. He was looking for the latest shares in WOBROLT, a Welsh soft drinks manufacturer, but couldn't find the information.
"We'll need some wine for this evening," suggested his wife.
"Yep," grunted Dave, not really listening.
"You do like Roderchot, darling, don't you?"
"Yep."
"There's still a loaf in the rucksack, isn't there?"
"Yep."

§

A tall dark man with lively brown eyes and a shiny bald head entered the shop through a side door, humming to himself. The woman was too focussed on her wine search to notice, but Dave, not renowned for tolerance, swiftly became annoyed by the joyful monotone and turned to offer his tormentor a suitable look of martyred annoyance. It didn't work; the man simply smiled, pleasantly, back at him; it was then that Dave realised ... 'he must be the proprietor.'
"You are English, yes?" asked the man.
"How could you tell?" laughed the woman. She left the oils of healthy lustre and concentrated on this fortuitous opportunity to flirt.
"It is a, how you say, look in your eyes that gave everything away," crooned the man. He'd heard her speaking to Dave from behind the thin plastic door.
'Wanker,' thought Dave, scanning the sport pages.
"Wow! your English is better than ours," said the woman, lazing over the counter top, her breasts wondrously revealed, her golden necklace jumping to attention.
"You are new to our country?"
"Oh, no, we've been coming here for years ... ever

since we won a two week holiday through a local radio pop quiz sometime in 1999. The locals are wonderful, sooooo laid back ... I've never met one quite like you though."
"Ah, pop quiz ... you mean music, yes? Do you know 'The Rascal', from Puentale Nalisha, our country's greatest rock band? They have many beautiful ... but best of all I like the dancing girls in their videos," confessed the shopkeeper.
"It's very quiet in here, even more than I recall ..." said the woman, trying to change subject.
"Today, Madam, the General is speaking. At least one person from every family must be available to hear what he says. Did you not hear of our recent independence?"
"No. Politics is boring," announced the woman - her name was Julie.
"That is so, Madam." He smiled and went on, "Now, would you have heard the joke about Mr. Politician and Mr. Shoemaker?"
"I ... I ... don't think so."
"Okay, is very funny. You laugh. I try and say all the parts in correct order. Politician and Shoemaker are travelling together on a ferry which connects the two mountainous sides of a central European river. Rough water. Nasty. Boat sets sail during ordinary working hours. There are no other passengers and the captain has gone below deck, to look through old bottle lids ... washed up beneath jetty while ship was in harbour. He loves things like that. He doesn't notice when a gang of pirates pulls up alongside his vessel and throw their grappling irons aboard. Silly idiot. Pirates, though, aren't stupid. They know it's not worth the trouble. They leave Captain Crosshatch to his misery and kidnap the lawmaker and the cobbler. Sensible move. Good shoes and big ransoms. Eventually they - Politician and Shoemaker - are tossed into a deep canyon from which there is no possible means of escape. Armed guards keep watch ... tough fuckers. Even so, they only seem to be around for two days out of five and appear quite

generous, bringing food, books and drink as an aid to the prisoners' survival. Surprisingly, considering the good conditions, both prisoners want to get away. They're bored. Mr Politician makes the first move. He engages a guard in a statistics-based conversation, all about the effect an individual's criminal behaviour can have on future generations of his family. The other guard is jealous. He wants to be involved. He crumbles a biscuit between his fingers and throws the dust at Mr Politician. Then he hurls an old suitcase over Mr Shoemaker's head. Big mistake. Later, after guard has gone to sleep, the shoeman rips open the case and finds a dozen suits of denim armour. 'Carraldo,' he thinks, 'I can escape.' He knots the clothes together, wakes Mr Politician, and tells him what's going on. Politician is happy but he wants to go first. He promises the shoemaker a monopoly on council workers footwear supply contracts once he's elected, and begins to climb the rope. Strange situation. Politician thinks, perhaps, like a builder who believes because he's built the odd Lego lighthouse, that he can also construct perfectly respectable two mile viaducts and full size presidential palaces. Naturally, he falls off the rope almost killing himself. The shoemaker laughs. When he's finished laughing he nurses the politician back to good health and, within a week, they're both climbing the denim tower, swapping jokes and exchanging phone numbers. Mr Politician though, is badly traumatised. After leaving the pit he gives up his former life and becomes an assistant to the shoemaker, mending sandals at a workshop in Tesekrilchen."

"So, what was the joke then?" asked Julie.

"Jokes, you should know, have a different meaning in our country to what they have in England," explained the shopkeeper, through howls of burning laughter.

"Are you happy about independence?" Their host wrinkled a silvery eyebrow and smiled.

"Of course. Who would not love freedom."

§

The General paused briefly as he passed the forty-first cage. A woman peered out at him. She looked horribly malnourished. Herbion La Vellempia, the prison's ruling officer, had noticed his superior's expression. He responded by straightening his collar until it was in a position which would place him beyond reproach. As they continued along the rows of identical misery cubes, butterflies ceased to flutter in La Vellempia's stomach. Perhaps the General wouldn't say anything. Maybe he had tougher lambs to boil.

"She didn't look especially healthy," murmured Malverzeign.

"Which one was that, Sir," asked La Vellempia.

"The black-haired girl in 41. I'm amazed she could still stand."

"There's been a small problem with catering lately, General. One of the men went down with food poisoning and was forced to throw away eleven sacks of ginger eclairs ..."

"Food poisoning might improve some of these wretches," sighed Malverzeign, grimacing.

'And how would you know,' thought La Vellempia, daydreaming of the vineyard at Vallicasion, of childhood memories ... hiding amongst leaves and berries before his friends came to visit then leaping out at them on arrival.

"You should be more careful, man. I'm deadly serious. I want that woman fed and clothed within the hour!"

"But there's men here in a worse state!" protested La Vellempia. "Damn the men," muttered Malverzeign, trying to remember President McMallon's telephone number.

§

The two men had been friends and allies for the past nine years. Malverzeign's business interests were the link which had brought them together, but the

President was always changing his email address ... an infuriating habit. Auransantia's put-upon premier needed both links but had neither. He didn't want to ask the President of Inner Zosherland again. A direct line to McMallon was crucial to discussions around the new facilities for his country's military personnel at their main European base on South Prasancilliar, not to mention the small matter of sixteen teenagers who'd been diverted away from summer camp to experience the pleasure of visiting McMallon in his own country. Little did they know of the experiments to come.

§

"I think you'll agree we've worked wonders with the ladies' wallpaper," said La Vellempia, pointing out the diagonal green stripes and pink terrapins on the walls of cell number five. This 'en-suite residence', although miniscule, was supposed to house at least half-a-dozen prisoners. However, due to the recent release of five suspected 'union militants' from the thirteen strong hand-scarf weavers guild, only one 'fallen woman' now remained. She wore her loneliness well; tall, respectably dressed, an individual with short, nicely layered brown hair, and thin lips which curled into a snarl as the General did his rounds.
"Hmmm, very nice, so long as the inmates had nothing to do with this."
"What do you mean, Sir," blurted La Vellempia, puzzled as to what harm it could do for prisoners to temporarily forget their predicament.
"It's vital they should never learn how to express themselves," hissed the General. It was a final statement. It hung in the air like factory smoke on a humid day. Neither man spoke as they saluted the guard and emerged into hazy sunshine.

§

Osijaz Villa, twelve miles east of the island's capital city, bore no resemblance in real life to its representation in the estate agent's window. There was no swimming pool. There were no cocktail cabinets. Yes, there was a 'sweeping view', but this was due more to the tendency of local women to get their brooms ready at the barest hint of an opportunity than it was to the expected vistas of sand, sea, and simmering white yachts. And, as promised, the building was unique. It consisted of two grey rectangles clumsily moulded together in the not-so-distant past, each resembling a loaf of unwanted bread whose hurried purchase had led to an inevitably brutal decay in the cupboard while other less deserving items were scoffed at a delirious speed. Tastefully open-planned was another pre-purchase description. It was really a polite way of saying 'the windows are yet to include glass and we couldn't be bothered building any interior walls'.

§

"Oh well, at least we can play indoor badminton," said Julie.

"Which'll be useful when there's no beds to sleep on," replied Dave, looking sad.

"We could invite the neighbours round to play. It'll be a good way of getting to know them," added Julie. But Dave wasn't listening. He'd begun circumnavigating the room in slow, measured, strides, as if to satisfy himself there was nothing wrong with the floorboards. In tune with this melancholy march was the sound of children playing football in the dusty roadway outside, oblivious to the arrival of yet more weather-worn, would-be entrepreneurs intent on their fragile slice of heaven.

§

Dave suddenly felt as though he was among them. His mind slipped back to that youth cup final seventeen summers before, the very day he'd met Julie. His team, Barningswood Ravens, had lost 3-2 in extra time. As he'd walked off the muddy field a pretty young girl wearing too many necklaces had bounced over to say 'Hello' and 'Goodbye', and in-between, 'Did you know that Dad's a scout for Cavenham Town and he thinks you're the best schoolboy player in Europe!' It was an act of elegant embroidery. Julie's father had once coached a local primary school team, but was more famous for uber drinking sessions, big hair and the fact that he was, then, serving a six year sentence for fighting, tax evasion and passport fraud; a hat trick of crimes. They all sounded pretty glamorous to Dave. By the following Saturday he'd asked his new admirer for a date.

§

"With any luck we'll get a refund," he said. Gloomy. Julie, meanwhile, was trying to smile for both of them.
"Oh, come on, it's what we've always wanted. A slower pace of life ... away from crowded pavements and freezing winters. I mean, yeah, it's hardly a palace but just look at all the potential! This house is like playdough. We can make anything out of it!"
"Playdough? Yeah, the original version was probably made of Blu Tac. I bet they ran a design competition at the local infant school."
"I just knew you'd be like this!" she yelled, hoping the neighbours would hear. Dave shrugged. He walked over to a fridge which appeared to be ploughing a lone furrow as the building's only mod-con. He opened the door and looked inside. His body shook slightly and then, as if injected with electrical current, jumped high into the air, leaving a shower of coins and a trio of murky receipts competing for space on the tiled flooring.
"What's wrong now?" said Julie in a tired voice.

"Bloody hell!" replied Dave, his finger guiding her eyes to a black chasm populated by two arrows and a slender bow. On closer inspection a note could be seen impaled on one of the arrows. It read, 'In defence of the hidden nations'.
"Is this meant for us to use?" Julie thought aloud, gingerly caressing the weapon as she spoke.
"I bloody hope not. I would have said it's some kind of old Auransantian custom, revived in recent times by a particularly patriotic national leader," remarked Dave.
"Or ... it could just be a silly joke ..?"
"Right. I'm going to unpack before the roof falls in."

§

Most of Dave's clothing had been squashed into the main green rucksack along with Julie's, and apart from a couple of tattered science fiction novels, three t-shirts salvaged from the rubbish and several stuffed animals of dubious design, there was little else to be concerned with. He pawed wearily at one of the books, stifling a groan.
"Oh, I've had enough of this. You can mope around and worry about Amelinta all you like but I'm going out to enjoy myself," said Julie.
"I'm not remotely bothered about Amelinta. She can eat grass and sit in a puddle for all I care."
"I don't believe you."
"I can't help that."
"You went on about her for hours last night."
"Oh, that ... that was only because she looks so much like the woman on reality TV who had that awful coathanger accident."
"Anyone would think you'd actually seen her, to hear the way you talk."
"She's in all of us, Jules. You, me, the stairs, the walls, a rock on the side of a lonely mountain in San Pellosia."
At this Julie rocked her head energetically from shoulder to shoulder blade, and fastened her dress.

She had a venue in mind and left the room.

§

Inside, on the turntable of opportunity - a crumbling former bakery on the outskirts of Mirvalla - sixteen thousand noisy islanders were keeping up the whisper to end all discreet conversations. They'd gathered to surrender their alcohol. This, in turn, would be exchanged for transmitters to receive the delights of SUPETV, a well-loved coastal delicacy. Kelvina Mirrbow, the station's founder, had persuaded an initially sceptical government of the drink's amnesty worth and was now seeing huge benefits in the form of public trust fund grant awards, ie money. A banquet of societies had been planned for the evening and Kelvina was trying, with little success, to look 'soulfully untidy' when she spied the President's familiar sun-kissed forehead easing through the crowd.

"Hello, Kelvina. To what do I owe this unexpected pleasure?" said the great man.

"Greetings, noble benefactor ... the joy is all mine. I don't mean to intrude or waste your valuable time but, as you know, I am presently enjoying a week's holiday, and yesterday lunchtime I happened to catch a slice of SUPETV while sipping a cocktail on the porch. What I saw disturbed me. The programming bore virtually no resemblance to the schedules me and Cassey had devised ..."

"That's right. I shouldn't overly concern yourself. It's easily explained. Although I, and indeed everyone else in the government believe the standard of programmes to be very high, we felt it simply wouldn't be suitable for the majority of the audience. Too highbrow. Insufficient reflection of market values. Come on ... even you must admit ... the lack of pointless game shows, one dimensional soap characters and documentaries proving the full worth of indiscriminate slaughter at suitable points in world history, is, quite frankly, worrying ..."

"But, Sir, it was always my intention ..."
"... therefore I have decided to place SUPETV in the capable hands of Jastervin Hopning, Chief Executive of the universal phenomenon that is InfiniTV. Jastervin's a remarkable man. He knows exactly how to move with global trends and also has the requisite clout to attract famous names to the proudly independent world of Auransantian visual entertainment."
"Jastervin Hopning? I thought he was still in jail?" Said Kelvina, quietly, more to herself than anyone. She couldn't process her thoughts. The room, and everything in it, was spinning. The President was smiling contentedly, like a man who'd just heard that his worst enemy's been arrested for a crime that he, himself, had committed. He ran his twisted, bony, fingers gently along Kelvina's arm.
"Indeed he was, my dear, indeed he was. But you know, sometimes it only needs one pillar in a hundred to fall and the whole bridge comes crashing down. The judge in question, a certain Caldirra Bennet, was found guilty of working with motives outside the public interest, and this I will not, under any circumstances, tolerate. Natural democracy must prevail. Following Bennet's conviction we conducted further research into all of our highest practitioners of law. You'd be amazed at our results. Levels of deviancy were astounding, and I have already taken steps to free all prisoners whose sentences were imposed by these scoundrels, on top of abolishing the entire criminal justice system as it now stands. Julie Cuadoras, an acquaintance from Great Britain, has been appointed head summariser of dispute. She's a gifted lady ... and a marvellous cook. Her role will be to finalise the paperwork in regards to internet locations.
"So, have I ... is that me, you know, sacked?" murmured Kelvina. The President laughed uproariously and clasped his previous favourite even more firmly about the arm.
"Of course not, my darling, what a suggestion! No,

you see, Julie hasn't let the ice cream melt about her feet. Your position has simply undergone an alteration. Instead of being the INTERNAL Chief Executive of SUPETV you are now the EXTERNAL face of the station, providing a welcome and, may I say beautiful, diversion for the world's media while promoting our noble shores on the international stage."
"Arggh." Kelvina winced as the truth sunk in.

§

Julie had been gone several hours and Dave, despite their recent troubles, had begun missing her. He liked a good argument before bedtime. He'd tried disagreeing with himself but it wasn't the same. His wife's sharp tongue, blazing cheeks and flashing talons were sorely missed. He hoped that wherever she was she'd kept her angry voice silent. A classic example of Julie's combative nature had occurred in March of the previous year. They'd gone out after work; a rainy, miserable, evening. Dave had chosen an Indian restaurant on Mayflower street as the venue for their eleventh wedding anniversary. A genial, white-shirted host had met them at the door.

§

The dining hall was a delight. Romantically lit, dripping with promise. The only other customers were a prim and serious looking couple in their late fifties, a single mother whose two young children were trying to build a town hall of menu cards, and two large, ostentatiously side-burned, men. The latter sat sprawled on a nearby sofa. They talked, laughed and whispered at a less than sociable volume. After Dave and Julie had eaten their meal, in that horrible period of unease when neither could decide whether to pay the bill or order something for dessert, he noticed her staring intently at the men and twitching her eyebrows in the way she always did when puzzled

or annoyed.
"Alright, Jules?" he asked, worried the men would see her glaring at them.
"D'you think they're drug dealers?" she replied.
"No ... and it's hardly our business if they are."
"I'm going to ask them," she said. Rising from her seat she marched purposefully over to the window - a decisive move. She wore a lacy white dress, high heeled shoes and silver earrings. She was clearly more exciting than their topic of conversation.
"Excuse me, I just wondered if you happened to be drug dealers?"
Dave buried his face in the turquoise tablecloth. There was no response. The men were either speechless, besotted or offended in the extreme.
"I SAID, are you two DRUG DEALERS?" she yelled. The furniture rattled and a five-thousand-year-old Sumerian vase leapt from the mantelpiece and shattered into a million pieces on a dangerously serious, middle-aged lady's rectangular head. There followed a moment of precious, gorgeous, silence until pandemonium took over. Startled junior chefs cascaded from the kitchen wielding graters, knives or spoons. The woman's husband rushed across to have a 'word' with the two men.
"What on earth are you doing conducting your seedy little business transactions in this restaurant?" he said, slowly. They ignored him, locked in their own private feud. Julie, meanwhile, had melted quietly into the background, trying to extract the contents of each man's pockets with the aid of a long-ish umbrella handle she'd found standing in the corner. It took seven policemen, when they arrived some nine minutes later, to clear the scene of fighting waiters, wailing co-owners, vengeful women and bewildered onlookers. One of the children didn't want to be left out. He wagged his finger at a policeman and pretended to list the irate officer's supposed crimes.

§

In Auransantia, Dave watched a cruel sun slip down over darkening sea and waited. Seconds dragged by. No news. His phone was useless and he could hear what he thought was thunder in the distance. He ran outside. Coming closer, their wings laden with missiles of every description, was a flock of screaming aeroplanes. The pilots' faces displayed no expression and, emblazoned on the lower tail of each aircraft a picture of an old fashioned looking gentleman and his own beloved wife imposed colour on the greying scene.

Dave fainted.

A Calmness all of her own.

Austere Herrington Junction, where the mighty Z9698 motorway led onto Chrissie Hanley's suspension bridge then on towards the estate agents' Republic of Ireland, had been shrouded in completely unnecessary sunshine for the past seven-and-a-half hours. Unnecessary, that is, for Aimee Chillbourne, huddled in a tiny pyramid shaped toll booth thirty yards above the black expanse of tarmac known formerly as Sandlecoombe Vale.

§

The place made her ill, dulled her senses and twisted her heart. The seven years that had passed since Aimee's re-invention as a living, breathing, sighing, dancing, eating, reading traffic light now felt like a dozen centuries, a baying army of sadomasochistic seconds. The job had shaped her in much the same way an ocean shapes delicately sculpted islands, leaving a beautiful shiny cliff seeming eternally content, but ready to fall apart without the slightest warning. At first she'd resented being locked away from the world. It reminded her of the ninety naughty detentions she'd received at school and, along with that, the glowering indifference of various overstretched form teachers. Now though, she wasn't so sure. She was beginning to derive sordid pleasure at her isolation, not happiness - that was something quite different, but a shy contentment, a shameful sense that life could be worse. It was an infuriating feeling.

§

Wasps fascinated her. Those which had somehow slipped inside the cabin were no longer afraid of giant, stuffed, foam grasshoppers, their incessant buzzing now interpreted as hospitality and interest rather than warning signals mixed in with condemnation. What did the insects feel? Were they really concerned only with survival and propagation or was that merely a side issue, a vital by-product of their true desires? Perhaps they enjoyed watching television. Maybe the reason hoverflies didn't write stupid articles comparing Erica Neillbey (from Emmerdale's psychosis) with Hercule Poirot, was that they recognised a pointless ritual when they saw one. Humans would always be available for the task. A possible explanation was that the General Council of Insect Deputies had programmed the mind of every person on earth to act in exactly the manner the magnificent bee-bee-3 required! Self indulgence in the culinary field was also an occupational perk. Aimee ate what she liked. She scalped pineapples, licked wagon wheels, and drained copious amounts of bacon juice into her eager mouth. It was a brutal regime. Occasionally crumbs would go to passing birds that took her fancy, their beaks raised in imitation of gods wanting an industrial sacrifice to secure the continued justification of corporate existence.

§

She waited for the next supercar. There had been none the previous fifteen minutes, thanks to a bizarre superstition which had recently engulfed west country motorists, and she wondered whether it was time for her to get behind the wheel again. Show her class. Three year driving bans were normally handed out only to those convicted of manslaughter. Aimee's particular crime - that of using a mobile phone whilst in the driver's seat - seemed fairly innocent, given that the vehicle wasn't moving at the time ...

§

"Two children, two dogs and a bottle opener," said a grumpy driver as he pulled up to the booth. She didn't recognise him. He was wearing a green blazer, orange tie and half-moon sunglasses, his hair gingery and slicked back in the conscientious manner of all who like to give the impression their lives are too rapid and successful for everyday trivia.

"That's okay, Sir, we don't charge for dogs," said Aimee, coming back down to earth, and speaking deliberately slowly.

"I would if I were you. That's no way to run a business," growled the man, handing over £16.00 for person-pluscar charges.

"Thank you for the advice. You can be sure I'll note it in the customer comment book," replied Aimee, hoping her sarcasm would quickly rid her of the man, to whom she'd taken an immediate, and perhaps slightly unfair, dislike.

"Don't bother. Now, you look like a sensible young girl. Could I perhaps trust you with the bottle opener?" He pulled a tiny corkscrew from his breast pocket. The rusted metal was attached to an elegantly carved kingfisher whose mad eyes suggested that wine had got to it.

"Doesn't he like the weather in Ireland?" asked Aimee.

"Last year I took the wretched device all the way to Karachi and was almost refused sandwiches at a bread stall. They did, eventually, let me have some tomato puree with chicken whispers, but it just didn't taste the same as Branzalamp. No tang. However, and I can support this with witnesses, the corkscrew performs magnificently within England's borders. I could name a thousand examples, all with their own specific quality, but I suppose the most telling intervention occurred at High Wycombe in 1984. You won't remember 1984 ... a funny year it was. The proles were putting up a last stand at the Pitheads, and Eastenders was barely a twinkle in a programming executive's eye. I'd just been promoted. My company valued me. I was returning from a business meeting in Lichfield City, relying on the motor rather than BR's dirty trains, and stopped for a doughnut on the Beaconsfield road. I got out the car, struggling a bit because of cramp, you know, and headed for a co-op supermarket lurking behind some trees ... I'm not usually a fan but beggars can't be choosers. The sliding door wasn't working properly, despite a sign saying OPEN TWELVE HOURS DAILY, and everything was dark inside. Suddenly all the lights flashed on, then went off, then came on again ... they were either having a disco or the place was being burgled. I tugged at the door and, as though an alarm had sounded in Brackmoor Fire Station, four girls swung down from the ceiling, laughing at me. Very disrespectful. All wore co-op uniforms, and all were on strike. I would have walked away there and then but something about them captivated me ... and it isn't what you're imagining. None of them were what I'd call glamorous. They wore weird, ghostly make-up and had ridiculous tatoos on their arms. They wouldn't stop laughing. This unnerved me and in the end, despite my curiosity, I had to turn back to where my car was parked; a blue Citroen if you're interested. I can tell that you are. Snow was falling on the bonnet. Hardly out of the ordinary you might say, after all it was mid-December, but I beg to differ. Bare, dry, roads and pavements surrounded my car ... like an enormous swiss roll that had been skimmed. The block in which snow was falling barely covered six square feet all round, although how low the seemingly invisible clouds were was all but impossible to judge. Having stared in wonder at the newly formed gathering of snowflakes I began to feel very warm and, acting on impulse, grabbed a handful of wet snow and retraced my steps to the co-op. Four people now stood at the window. A middle-aged man had joined the girls and everyone was laughing. I took steady aim, and drawing my arm back to its full length hurled an ice bomb at the unsuspecting picket line. Bizarrely, the glass seemed to expand on impact, as if reaching out for the snowball, and all of the staff had vanished into thin air. When I reached the point where my missile had landed, a small wooden cardboard-like box lay beneath the window. I'd

expected to find snow. On closer examination I found the box was decorated with countless mysterious inscriptions, all facing a representation of the moon at it's centre; most intriguing. Two days later, on December 19th, 1984 to be exact, I took my present to the ancient history section at Luttledean museum and showed it to an elderly director by the name of Jerry Tickson. Old Ticksey, as I grew to call him after we'd become friends, was astonished by the randomness of my discovery, but even more enthralled by the object itself. He'd struck gold, silver and bronze all at once. To him, and to a thousand specialists of similar persuasion in universities from Honduras to Macedonia, the box was living proof that Sumerian breakfast cereal packaging had predated Kellogs' modern capitalist orthodoxy by well over six thousand years. I, in turn, gained my own small measure of satisfaction in relation to the find. I was awarded an honorary degree by Oxford University. In addition to this and, I confess, trumping it, the British Government gave me four million pounds to invest in my own printing company. "So, instead of you paying a bribe for the privilege, I'm supposed to accept a fairy story about lucky corkscrews, risking my job in the process," said Aimee.
"If you want to put it in that cynical way," shrugged the man, wiggling Wycombe's favourite bottle opening kingfisher before her eyes.
"Alright then ... I suppose it'll be company for the wasp," she replied, taking the bird by its chestnut stockings.
"I'll be back a week on Thursday," said the man. His engine fired. A cloud of sherbet - remains of Aimee's six o' clock drinks break - flew up from the road and floated around for a while, clearing only once the car had disappeared from view.

§

"Well, I doubt we'll be seeing him again," said Aimee to the wasp as she sank her sturdy frame into the comfy chair. Now, privacy guaranteed, she allowed her mind to wander over pre-interruption areas. A vicious scowl reflected her mental anguish. Her line of thinking was heading towards the Judge and whether or not she took pleasure in sentencing innocent victims of modern society, who were after all only trying to compete on an uneven playing field in a world which valued competition and envy above all else. There was nothing to eat for lunch - Aimee having forgotten to pack her sandwiches again, so she decided to go for a walk in the sparsely wooded space nearby, a perk of the job. Even if another vehicle did appear there was a six foot steel barrier in place to hold it up until she arrived. Suitably reassured and daintily coiffured, she strolled to the valley's edge and filled her lungs with air. A horn sounded.

"Fuck."

She rushed back to the kiosk like a frontline grand prix commentator and waited for the distant monstrosity to appear. The driver didn't hurry. His car was green, low, and covered in white patches which could not have been there - either intentionally or accidentally. They seemed to follow no particular pattern and Aimee, who prided herself on not being completely ignorant when it came to motor cars, supposed that the vehicle must have been made on the continent. What continent, though, she couldn't possibly say.

§

The driver took an age winding down his windscreen. It was as though he was afraid of being recognised. When he did eventually show his face an involuntary shiver snaked up her spine. The man's eyes, nose and mouth had been pushed inside his head, creating the impression of a bowl hanging on someone's kitchen wall. There were unsightly yellow blotches all over his neck and arms, barely concealing an old, military style t-shirt at least seven sizes too small.

"I would have apologised in advance for my appearance but this morning, you see, I was expecting to make the journey by train," said a pleasant, though unexpectedly feminine voice. The man was attempting to smile and Aimee immediately felt embarrassed at her reaction.

"I'm sorry, Sir, it's just that hardly any cars have come through today and your app ... er, arrival, came as something of a shock."

"My face looks like it's been used as a football by four competing herds of wildebeest ... I know that. However, there is a reason ... if you've time to hear a little story?" He lisped politely, handing over a fistful of change. Aimee gazed up at a cloud of swans drifting across the endless gray sky, stared at the vast ocean of deserted highway, nodding agreement. It seemed to be a day for stories; besides, she could count the change while he talked.

§

"Well, it's difficult to know where to begin but the story goes like this. I used to live in a little town called Skellsmere, on the east coast of England it was. It had six pubs, a weekend market, a co-op, a football ground and a ruined fishing industry. I liked it but had to leave. Having received my degree in Geology at the University of Erringbay I was fortunate to have been offered a job working alongside a scientific team located in Herringwood-on-Sea. I grabbed the opportunity with both hands. My parents were only a half-hour drive away and there were several other pockets of relatives and former college acquaintances scattered within a radius of about fifty miles. In some ways they were almost too close, though I didn't want to let go completely. Anyway, things were going well, better than I'd expected. I'd made some new friends and the work was reasonably interesting. What more can you ask? Me and another recent university graduate, Alex Finningstone, were set to work in the laboratory where we spent many gruelling hours analysing the strong, near translucent liquid which our field workers had extracted from the cliffs at Tormegor Head. As our studies progressed we realised that an earlier explanation, given by Alex I might add, was proving hopelessly inadequate at solving the mystery. This idea was based largely on previous experiences of such phenomena, holding that the blood of a long extinct species of animal had mingled with a galaxy-defying chemical in the rock to produce something resembling a kind of weak, blackcurrent-flavoured glue ..."

Aimee should have been outraged at the man's disregard for her input, but instead found herself staring at his car and wondering which had come first, the wheel or the wedding ring?

"No Hilvasarzeen X was identified in any of the samples ... a small point, you could say, but a crucial one, given the genetic make-up of certain Obrasseedical creatures. Argh, you look confused! Okay, I'll elaborate. By Obrasseedical I mean the era of unidentified animal gentry said to have preceded the sacking of Rome in 411 AD. No skeletons or preserved carcasses have survived into the modern world. It's a huge problem. A site at an old swimming pool in Bratislava is the next great hope, or potential catastrophe - depending on how you look at it. I'm not convinced. Now, where was I? Oh, yes, Alex and his plans. He was very upset when the team rejected his hypothesis ... surprising, when you consider that setbacks happen all the time. We accepted failure. We knew it's importance to our job. Alex, by contrast, was spending an increasingly enormous slice of his day in the laboratory, where he laboured on insignificant side-projects and talked nonsense to the bunsen burners. His social circle had diminished to a unit of one. Maybe he was afraid that our 'questioning approach' might contaminate him. A month passed in much the same way and it was clear something needed doing. His obsessive attention to the most irrelevant detail was hampering our work, causing the whole chain to corrode and disintegrate. Yet, everyone liked him. He'd been so dedicated and humorous in the beginning and no one wanted to hasten his demise. Our boss, a small, shy, middle-aged man called Villmer Granchyre decided to solve the problem in a mature and intellectually rigorous way. We drew lots. I lost. I was now expected to formulate a plan for Alex's dismissal. I managed to negotiate the arrival of a new graduate, Kelly Sanquecha, in Alex's place, at the same time providing the latter with a supply of castor oil, tomato juice and broscolyde to study as though it were fresh from the rocks at Tormegor head. This he took with good grace, which only served to underline the extent of his delusions. It created a terrible moral dilemma. Was it better to balloon a sick man's sense of purpose or should we simply have stated our doubts in a plain and open manner at the risk of causing greater trauma than would otherwise have been necessary?

§

The man was gesturing so wildly with his stubby little hands that Aimee was forced to duck. She feared a stray nail in the eyeball. None of the rabbits seemed perturbed however, and several of them had edged closer, as if to eavesdrop.

"Two weeks had passed and everybody had noticed a slight change in Alex's demeanour. Nothing much, but the signs were certainly there. He'd begun passing salt across the dinner table again. He'd nod vague greetings at mealtimes. He'd even engaged a senior lecturer in conversation about the relative merits of parsley or cinnamon in fried ostrich casampa. Things were looking up. Then, while I was engaged at my work in the laboratory one morning, sixteen test tubes containing traces of the recently

sampled red mixture exploded, and everything in the world turned green. I was convinced of my own consciousness and yet, although my body was perched on two feet and moving, it was all false. I saw grasshoppers. I saw spongehoofed friesians bouncing up and down before an audience of collapsing yellow ice creams spewing out regiments of ants, ants, ants ... and more dishcloths. When I recovered after three months of comatose inertia, they found me a job at the high school in Nexellton. I was forbidden from contacting the institute. They said it would harm my recovery. I pretended to go along with this plan, and indeed the school teaching was enjoyable, taking up more time than I'd imagined, but every weekend at first light I pulled on a simple disguise and travelled by train to the Lincolnshire coastline. Centuries may have passed. Entire streets had been closed down and the only remaining shop was a monolithic Tesco supermarket which looked like a hotel for football managers, and footloose undertakers scared of woodworms lurking behind pictures of Arundel's golden meadow ..."
"Didn't this bloke, Alex or whatever his name was, have something to do with the explosion?" asked Aimee, catching up.
"Arggghh, now, that's the strange thing! When I arrived at the institute Kelly Sanquecha greeted me almost as though I'd been expected, and led me inside to meet the others - Professor Murcheston, Graham, Sally, Liam and Fiona. We chatted about the old times then the subject got around to Alex. Here, Sally, who'd always been the best mediator, took over and informed me that Alex had suffered such trauma after the accident that he'd thrown himself off the cliffs at Solgerdeen caravan park and landed, knees first, in the sand below. Somehow, and it was described as miraculous on BBC radio Lincolnshire, he'd survived but with two broken legs, a shattered pelvis and the loss of a stranger's house keys. Later, he went to live in South Wales. He was last known to have been running a cotton reel collector's sanctuary

in Dunmarvey, West Ireland ..."
"And I suppose that's where you're going?" said Aimee.
"Of course," replied the man.
"Innocent or guilty?"
"I hope so. What do you think?"
"I think you're mad ... and you've given me too much money; I only need a tenner."
"I know. The rest is a bonus," smiled the man, thrusting a small plastic dog into Aimee's hands.
"I'll take it this isn't a gift," sighed the toll girl.
"I'm afraid not. He's a loyal friend. I don't want to run the risk of losing him in Ireland."
"Fair enough."
"I'll pick him up on the way back. Shouldn't be too long. Do you know where the next roadside cafe is?"
"No, no, not really. I try not to worry about that side of the border."
"Understandable," mumbled the man. He then drove off with a graceless clattering of unprotected fanbelts and a wounded accelerator pedal. A yellow car Followed immediately in his wake, driven by a heavily tanned young man leaning out the window, only stopping at the very last moment, narrowly avoiding a disastrous collision with the concrete barriers.

§

"Hi gorgeous, do you sell pizzas?"
"No ... believe it or not. This is a toll booth. I sell permits for travel to idiots who want to cruise up and down the highway."
"You must have something special about you then ... to land a job like this." He looked no older than fifteen or sixteen. His eyes - like large grey saucers - were focusing on the pattern of ugly, mock-snooker blinds decorating the cabin roof.
"I've lost my keys, further back down the road ... I'll have to try and find them before anyone else does," he said, with a coy smile.

"Well, you might be better off paying first," noted Aimee.
"No, no, there's no time to lose and, besides, they could be twenty miles away by now."
"You haven't got any money, have you?" guessed Aimee with a smug voice, nauseating even herself. She'd always wanted to say that, but because of the dreary efficiency of her nation's drivers she'd never had the chance. Now, miraculously, such an opportunity had arrived. Whispering sweet lullabies. She couldn't hide from responsibility or pass the blame. How would flashy Fernando get out of this one?
"I dropped a map out of the window as well. Careless. It's a very detailed, large-scale one of the area around a house I've got to find in Ireland," he said, pathetically.
"I've got thousands in the cabin, Ordnance Survey, they're pretty good," lied Aimee in the manliest voice she could muster.
"No thanks. I'm not sure any of them will have quite the same personal touch and delicate vulnerability."
"Is that a bad thing?"
"I, er, dunno ..."
"Fine. Go and retrieve them but don't be long. The border shuts in a few hours' time."
"Can I leave the car with you? I think I stand more chance of finding it if I walk along the verge."
"If you want. It looks in need of a good rest."

§

Fifteen minutes later the young man had vanished, the only other sign of life being a wounded toad gamely trying to lead her teenage offspring across the highway. They'd leap ahead then she'd draw them back, either in fear for their safety or because she didn't want to be the last to see an epiphany of squandered heroism. Minutes drifted by. Hours scuttled into the distance. And still her customers remained silent. She amused herself drawing pictures on a sheet of mouldy cardboard that had been hiding under the desk. She had little option; her food supplies were running low. The hopeful squiggles soothed her, adding poetry to her plight. She sketched the contours of a friendly monster's back then dignified his obese frame with a scarlet nightgown, a flowing orange scarf, and a pair of waterproof fishing boots eleven sizes too small. His freshly-painted eyes met her own. They offered no thanks, no redeeming hint of gratitude; instead, they laughed. She was disappointed with her creation. She snapped the pencil in two, cheering joyously as it cracked, and proceeded to search for the IN EVENT OF DISASTER handbook which she knew to be lying somewhere in the cabin. Before she could find it a police car drew up. Her friend, Dave, wound down the window.

"Alright Aims?" he growled.

"Not bad, thanks. You?"

"Surviving. Just. Today was supposed to be my day off, Bloody Darren's ill again though, ain't he, so Sergeant Miles said I ought to come in. Bloody waste of time. Town's dead and even the lager smugglers are keeping their noses clean. You seen anything?"

"Hardly ... a couple of cars, nothing else."

"Poor 'ol girl. You must get bored in there!"

"Oh, well, y'know, I do my best to stay busy. Mrs Percy lent me a book to read and Neil Ruthingford gave me some pens and ..."

"Yeah? What do you write?"

"I don't. I draw"

"Can I see one of your pictures?"

"No way. Too embarrassing."

"Come on, I ..."

"N-o ..."

"Okay, okay, you win. I won't push my luck. Oh, by the way, have you got any aspirins?"

"Sorry, I finished them off this morning ..."

"Typical. Never mind, I'm used to suffering in silence. I'll pick up a packet at Colin's office on the ride home.

See ya."
"Bye," called Aimee. The patrol car slipped from her orbit. He was heading deeper into England and she could see his future. It involved chip sandwiches, rationed sex, and drab holidays in the mid-market section of the international tourist empire. She kept all the lucky charms.

She never saw the salesman or the geologist again.

A different coloured dress might have been advisable. Red was, after all, very much in vogue at the time. It would have been far more effective at disguising the various blood, wine and tomato stains that Kathy's garment had allowed itself to acquire; so embarassing. Her cream cocktail spectacular now looked more like a butcher's overcoat.

§

"Who've you been slaughtering today then, Kate ... critics or authors?" asked Stanley Gayse, the company's dangerously rotund and pathetically unfunny chief executive.
"Neither. It's the latest fashion actually, NEZ RE COIR, all the way from Gredzavia; dates back to the early fifteenth century. It was originally developed as a means by which intelligent, semi-educated women could protest against their exclusion from higher status colleges in the old Shrellandian empire," Kathy replied, fixing Stanley with a suitably disdainful glare.
"Full marks for effort. That's a wonderful and picturesque way of saying you can't control yourself any more than you can pick a dress properly," sneered Stanley before drifting off to a quieter corner of the smoke-filled room.
"Bastard," muttered Kathy. She hated these events; 'Snake bouquets' she liked to call them. Allegedly a method by which the 'Cym' publishing house authors and agents could meet to discuss matters literary and address editorial concerns. These meetings were actually a sham, a misty thin umbrella disguising a pointless preening and sartorial one-upmanship better suited to advertising billboards or upmarket neighbourhood watch galas. It wasn't as if any authors actually turned up. They were too busy sitting in dirty, chandeliered chambers or writhing in agony realising that their latest spurious analogy inflicted on

paper was little more than a reheated version of what had already appeared some fifty pages earlier.

§

Kathy was the 'writer's doctor'. Her job was to cajole these living legends into finishing their semi-coherent manuscripts whilst providing positive energy, pretty smiles and (mercifully) a metaphorical arm around the shoulder. Despite her generosity some remained dissatisfied. They didn't just want her arms across their necks, they wanted her fingers behind their jeans and her tongue in places it could never belong. Her boss, of course, was less than impressed when she complained.
"They're artists, darling, you can't expect them to behave like normal people," Sion had replied.
"They eat, drink and walk like everyone else don't they? They have the same needs, so they can live by the same rules!" responded Kathy. Sion laughed. Even so, although dismissive at the time he must have said something, because it wasn't long before the literary lechers abandoned their vulgar pursuits and shrank back to doing what they did worst. Kathy, meanwhile, remained on her guard. If she knew one thing it was that thriller writers never forget, especially those whose specialties lay in dissolving their real life enemies into fictional form.

§

Kix Michael was particularly notorious. The Australian fast-bowler-turned-science fiction-novelist had received more column inches on the release of one short story than he'd had in his entire fictional career when 'Zeyma's Prey' ... the story of a tennis player who is stalked then killed by an alien ... took on a vaguely autobiographical twist after Chester Zeyma, and old rival of Michael's, died unexpectedly on the very spot where he'd been struck by a falling meteorite. 'It happens' some people had said ... but

Elle didn't believe them. She suspected a curse. There was only one writer at Cym who Kathy really admired, and he wasn't there. He had his reasons.

§

Sydney Strake was no great fan of social gatherings, having been accidentally 'bashed' at one on his ninth birthday. He would usually be found somewhere between Mercon Wood and Hopsmere on the eastern bank of Pweltsgewer river. Here, he splashed ink, talked to fish and kept away from trouble; not that it kept away from him. That was the thing about being a slightly famous novelist. You could walk around the centre of a very large town in Kesvellaria and not be recognised until, suddenly, a dark street would reveal the obligatory discontented 'uber' fan. There he would be, sullen, ill dressed and socially inadequate, while their the author was nervous, thirsty and wishing he'd turned left outside the carrier bag museum. Kathy had always told Stanley to take such semi-stalker types as a compliment. 'They wouldn't be there if you weren't such a brilliant writer,' she'd say, and she meant it. Sidney's novels, largely set in Nedvar during the Roman occupation, were funny, vivid, humanistic and real enough for the reader to believe he was part of the story. This brought its own problems though. Strayke didn't realise how powerful his writing was, and as a consequence he suffered for it ... often. Guilt could be a terrible thing.

§

It was nearly midnight. Some of the early arrivals had already drifted away so Kathy grabbed a bottle of wine and collapsed gratefully onto the red velvet sofa. She'd earned her chocolates, done her best through an exhausting evening. Food fights,veiled threats, screeching agents and trophy dogs had all stolen their slice of the action, some having been more prominent

(annoying) than others. Relieved it was almost over but not willing to go home just yet, she supped the delicious, fruity wine and closed her eyes.
"Hello," he said, in perfect Mancunian English.
"W ... who are you?" murmured Kathy, wondering whether she was dreaming. The man was tall, with swept-back silver hair and a hook-like nose which didn't quite fit his profile. It was too wide, too crooked and too blotchy for such a gaunt, angular face. It might have been sewn on by an errant plastic surgeon after an accident involving chips, peas and Chinese fireworks.
"I'm your boss ... Ralph Jamieson," said the man, stretching out a hand.
"Eh ... no you're not. Michael Walton is my boss, has been for the last three years, and I've never seen you before in my life," replied Kathy, swiftly composing herself.
"Not any more sweetie. I'm in control now."
"Is this some kind of fucked up chat up line?"
"It can be if you want it to."
"The only thing I want ... is to get out of here," said Kathy, diving between the stranger's legs and making a run for the door. She felt sick. How much had she drunk? Michael, or whoever he was, barely moved a muscle and she was able to beat a hasty retreat through the front entrance. The security guard smiled as she passed him. She waved back, relieved to get away.

§

Only one other person was waiting for the 49 at the Sharlack Street bus stop. Late night strangers could be menacing and Kathy was relieved to see a familiar face, her workmate Maria Turner, grinning through the darkness as she crossed Percee Lane.
"I thought you'd pulled," said Maria, sliding over to make room on the corrugated iron bench.
"No such luck ... though I don't think I was far off," laughed Kathy. "I prob'ly shouldn't have had that

extra glass of wine. One bottle was enough. I ended up falling asleep on the sofa. When I finally woke up some weird bloke who looked like Count Dracula was there, insisting he was my boss. Very weird. A few dodgy comments later I was beginning to get seriously worried ... so I legged it through the building and here I am."

"Oh, and what exactly did this 'Dracula lookalike' say?"

"That his name was Ralph Jamieson and that, basically, he was in control."

"Oh dear," muttered Maria.

"What do you mean?"

"He is our boss. Michael's sold the business; apparently needed money in a hurry, and Dracula - as you call him - was the only one to make him a decent offer."

"How come I didn't know anything about this?" moaned Kathy as their bus came into view.

"Hardly anyone knew. I only found out the other day because I overheard Michael talking to Jamieson in The Joiners Tavern."

"What was he saying?"

"Just that everything was okay, no problems with the deal and all due processes had been followed. It all sounded pretty dodgy to me, but what can you do? If we confront him it's our jobs that'll be on the line."

"We could always go on strike," said Kathy brightly.

"How? Management doesn't recognise any union and I can't see us getting much support from the others," sighed Maria.

"You're right. I know you're right ... but we can't let it happen, we must find some way."

"Yeah, I agree, something needs doing. I just think we need more time to work out a strategy. Jamieson's got a terrible reputation y'know. Three of his previous companies have gone bust and there's a whole cavalcade of ex-wives and former financial associates pursuing him through the courts."

"Brilliant. So, if he goes under he'll take the company

with him!"
"Probably."
"Fuck!"

§

Kathy didn't get home until one a.m. She'd grabbed some chips from Maddies Fish Bar and was looking forward to eating them in front of the telly, surrounded by her father's dreary business magazines and their lodger's discarded sweet wrappers. Theirs was not a tidy household. It was hard to balance the demands of three very different people, so they'd compromised by letting each other do what they wanted, no questions asked. Not a perfect solution but it had certain merits.
"You're just in time," said a cheery female voice as Kathy tumbled in through the front door.
"For what?"
"For 'Jasmine Bleak, Supersleuth' of course," enthused Donna, squeezing up to make room for her on the sofa. It was a lose-lose situation. If Kathy went to bed she'd be unable to sleep, haunted by images of Jamieson's grinning face as he sent her company spinning into the abyss, and if she stayed there'd be two hours of an unnaturally enthusiastic seventeen-year-old to endure, along with Kesvellania's least convincing feminist detective. Upstairs seemed like a world away though, so she opted for the latter.
"Good day?"asked Donna. The opening credits rolled.
"Not really," replied Kathy, slumping sulkily into the velvet shrouded cushions.
"Want to talk about it?"
"No."
"I had a brilliant time in Cook's this 'arvo. Jenny Davies was there - y'know, that girl who went out with the antarctic survey team last year - and she told me loads of stuff about Abel Milde. Her cousin lives next door to him in Daisyvayne. He's such a freak. He's got a secret tunnel from his house to the shops

because he doesn't like being seen in public and, apparently, he keeps two zebras and a cheetah in his back garden," gushed Donna, seemingly mesmerised by the staid eccentricities of Zerraland's greatest living rock star.
"With his money I'd build a casino in the garden and invite six dozen Russian-speaking flamencos to the bloody place," scoffed Kathy.
"Just 'cos you're jealous."
"Of him? You must be joking"
"Are so."
"Am not!"
"Whatever," said Donna, smiling and returning her gaze to the screen. Jasmine Bleak, so called 'supersleuth' had tired of weaving elaborate tales for murder suspects and was instead staring dreamily into the eyes of a typically thick set, oily-haired private investigator.
"Gee, I wonder what's coming next," said Kathy sarcastically.
"She needs someone to help her solve the case doesn't she? I mean, two heads are better than one," protested Donna.
"Yeah, and the other head just happens to belong on the shoulders of someone who looks more like a catalogue model than a strangely talented policeman."
"He is pretty hot, I agree."
"Exactly. Have you ever seen a copper who looks anything like that?"
"I wish I had," replied Donna honestly. She hadn't enjoyed much luck with men in recent times. Her last boyfriend, a drug dealer called Jason, was in a juvenile detention centre after assaulting two traffic wardens; her infatuation with English teacher Martyn Byrd was still the talk of Soyadale College.
"You'll find someone," said Kathy kindly. She knew from experience that seventeen was a difficult, often embarrassing age, but she also knew that in the long run Donna shouldn't have too many problems finding a bloke. Her looks, for one, certainly didn't pose a

handicap. Donna was reasonably tall and slim, with just-below shoulder length hair, blue eyes and the kind of pert nose and mouth attractive enough to turn faces on earthquake-hit streets. She was a rarity in that her beauty defied fashion. She would have looked equally attractive in any country, setting or epoch of human history. Kathy, 26 years old and single since her boyfriend had left her to 'see the world' was glad she'd taken Donna in. She part-owned No. 7 Ryggar Street with her father, John, and they weren't always on the best of terms. She worked long hours in the Cym offices but she liked a home life as well and couldn't understand how her father, who ran his own sellotape business, managed to survive on three hours sleep a night and the sort of Salinger-esque social life characterised by your average North European spy colony. Donna was opposite. She had many friends, varied interests and was rarely home before nine in the evening.

§

After Donna's mother, Julia Oakes, had decided to leave town the previous May it seemed likely that her daughter would be travelling with her. Donna had never really contemplated living away from home before, didn't believe she'd ever want to, but, as the move drew closer had begun having second thoughts. She wasn't a child anymore. She was at college now, living in the place she'd called home since early childhood, and Erringby - more than anything or anywhere else - was where she wanted to stay. It suited her. Julia wasn't surprised when Donna confessed to her how she felt. She would have been the same at sixteen, friends around her and a settled place to live. She didn't break down in tears and beg Donna to go with her. She was only moving a few dozen miles and they'd still see plenty of each other. It was fine, really. So she gathered all her charm, asked the neighbours around, and was grateful when Katy Phillips said, "It would be nice to have another face at the dinner table."

§

The Pelican Grange cut a dashing figure, scything through the pearl blue waters of Zylanno harbour, rocking its passengers like marbles in a rotating hat. Huge red skies clung to the tooth-like ridge of Cranzour mountain, casting a blood-gray light on the sea. Far to the south, beyond leaping turquoise waves, a cream coloured ship blared its siren in a final call for evening tea.

"I bet their Salmon's not as fresh as ours," said a chubby elderly man, balancing a glass of champagne on his knee.

"I shouldn't think they've got horseradish sauce either," sang a heavily tanned woman beside him, perched on her ketchup-red lilo in the centre of the boat viewing area. The three other passengers looked content to sleep their way through the exchange.

"I'm not sure whether 'that lot' are going to have any dinner ..." said chubby - name of Kevin.

"Suits me, Kevvy," cooed his female companion. Patricia Duce was wearing a two piece green bikini, concealing skin that could at best be described as blotchy. Neither scarlet lipstick nor a chestnut fringe could disguise the lines on a face already hopelessly ravaged by the relentless march of time.

"You're looking nice, dear," said Kevin, not looking at his wife.

"I always do, don't I?"

"Oh, yes my darling ... especially on holiday. The Mediterranean sun always seems to bring out the best in you."

"It hasn't done much for them," laughed Patricia, nodding at their fellow passengers.

"Oh, I don't know. Look at 'em all, so content, thinking that because she's our only child she'll end up inheriting the family fortune thereby avoiding a life of pain and unrewarded labour. Fool. Martin, our poor little mechanic, escaping a miserable family,

believing his third-rate services to be invaluable during our voyage. He doesn't know I've got an engineering degree. The muppet. As for Ralph, well, the mind boggles ... it really does. How someone who's managed to worm his way into such a hefty fortune can fall for my simple stories is a mystery ... although maybe I don't give myself enough credit," mused Kevin, sipping at his dry champagne.
"You don't darling, you don't," agreed Patricia, kneading his arm as if it were a pastry tower.
"Always been my problem. Modesty."
"So, what are you intending to do with the little mites?" asked his wife.
"Martin must die. He's ignorant as sin but still knows too much. Ralph should be harmless under stricter controls. He's quite weak really, can't keep an opinion any longer than he can a glass of wine, so I don't think he'll be a problem long term. Ralph likes money, but he likes his cricket more."
"Don't we all."
"Not us, my darling, not us."

§

Monday mornings, never a happy time. Rain had almost swallowed Erringby the night before and a steady stream was still falling when Kathy jumped down from the Hayzire road tram. She braced her umbrella against the deluge. It clicked open at terrifying speed then acted like a sail, dragging her along Sebastian street to the Company offices.
"Nice evening?" asked Kayleigh, her secretary, once she'd collapsed at her desk.
"It might have been if Tony's 'spoonface' larch hadn't run into me at the bar," she replied. Kathy had spent much of the previous night at a 'Rosechain' concert, at Patti's Music Theatre. Although she'd enjoyed the lilting, bubblegum pop melodies she'd been less than charmed about running into one of her 'blind date' catastrophies from eleven months before. Theirs had not been a long acquaintance. Tony, not

his real name apparently, was at least fifteen years her senior, with a sunken, spoon-like face and the kind of low, robotic voice best suited for answerphones or radio station weather reports. They barely survived the first round of drinks.

"Oh yeah, what did he have to say for himself?" asked Kayleigh, a sucker for gossip of any kind.

"I don't know, I wasn't really listening ... something about shops? Oh, and he's left the ice cream industry and moved on to a 'new' challenge. He didn't say what."

"That all?" sighed Kayleigh, visibly disappointed.

"Pretty much."

"Some things never change."

"Nah ... he's got a new girlfriend though. Her name's Limollylla, a dentist, really weird by all accounts so they should get on well."

"Not Limollylla Simmons?" gasped Kayleigh, her bright eyes widening to near unmanageable size.

"That's right,"said Kathy, calmly.

"She was my sister's dentist. She took some of her teeth out last year, charged $20,000 for the privilege, and used painkillers about 300 percent stronger than was necessary. My sister slept for a week!"

"I'm surprised you noticed the difference," laughed Kathy. Kayleigh almost gave her an evil look at the clumsily worded joke-not-quite-aninsult, but knew her intentions were good, so before long they were both laughing; no better way to start a morning. By lunchtime Kathy had signed two rejection slips for manuscripts, the waste and cruelty already beginning to get her down. All the effort involved. All those carefully selected pronouns and vibrant, bouncing, paragraphs. How many good writers abandoned hope at the first rejection? Was it the truth, as Joe Strummer had said, that 'True talent will always emerge in time'? Kathy didn't know ... she wasn't even sure she wanted to know. A knock at her door? She stretched out, surprised, spilling coffee all over the company mailing list ...

"Damn," she said, and then, "Come in!"

"Hi," chirped Anthony Foyle, entering in a cloud of pre-heated air and expensive aftershave.
"Anthony ... just the person I wanted to see," lied Kathy, as her slightly older colleague sprawled on the comfy chair. Anthony meant well, with his eager dress sense and corporate handbook-lifted compliments, it was just that everybody found him extremely annoying.
"Don't worry ... it's pleasure, not business," he said confidentially, raising his left eyebrow in his typically creepy manner.
'Let me be the judge of that,' thought Kathy, already scared of what might be coming.
"Oh, yes," was her guarded response.
"Do you like horses, Kathy?"
"Sometimes," she replied, honestly.
"Sometimes?"
"When they're a safe distance away from me." This seemed to throw Anthony somewhat, suggesting, as it did, a certain lack of enthusiasm for one of nature's finest creatures, but after brief head scratching and a long, knowing glance at nothing in particular, he was soon back on the scent.
"As they are at most high security racing venues," he trumpeted.
"If you say so."
"There you are then. Perfect. Me, you, Eskyre racetrack, champers, betting slips, the smell of freshly mown grass. Friday, six pm, magnifico!"
"Are you asking me out on a date?" asked Kathy, incredulously, trying to imagine anything more repulsive.
"Absolutely," yelped the daring one.
"Okay."

§

It was crazy really, sheer insanity. She'd known the guy for two years and probably liked him less now than she had then. Which wasn't very much. She was walking home, waving at Mork's the newsagent, mulling over the decision in her head. Was she just bored? Did she think that by her going out with him Anthony would magically transform into a tolerable human being? Some hope. There was more chance of alligators growing wings or a toadstool becoming Prime Minister. No, she'd made her bed, now she'd have to lie in it. As long as she didn't have to lie there with him.

§

They were further out to sea now, drifting towards what they hoped would be a far more secure future. Filtered moonlight sparkled on scarlet decks, night jays squawked from inky skies and Ralph gulped down another glass of brandy while Martin nibbled on pine-needle biscuits nearby.

"Lovely night," said the latter.

"Beautiful ... and this is only the start. We're on the sherbet shuttle for glory, Marty, and no mistake!"

"Yes, it's unbelievable when you think where we were this time last year."

"Mulchmore prison, staring at a f***ing life sen tence!"

"Great building material, reinforced cork," laughed Martin.

"Especially during an earthquake," agreed Ralph, pouring a second glass.

"I wonder what happened to all the other prisoners?"

"To be honest, Marty, I don't give a f**k. We were there, and they were there; now we're here and they're wherever; the prison's gone and the money's ours. It all goes to prove one thing if you ask me ..."

"Oh yeah, what's that then?"

"You can't keep a good man down!"

"Too true." They both laughed. Two throaty chuckles echoing across a silent ocean. Martin turned and threw his remaining biscuits over the side, then lay back on the rock hard deck as though it were a sun lounger. Ralph followed suit.

"It'd be nice to see Jason again, eh?" said Martin.

"We will if he's got any sense. He ran the show in that place. No, don't you worry, Mart. If he's half as cunning on the outside as he was inside we'll be seeing Jason again, no doubts," insisted Ralph.
"You reckon?"
"Oh yeah, definite. I mean, the rich and powerful do tend to keep similar company, don't they?"
"I suppose."
"Exactly. Today, cruising the world; tomorrow, running the bloody place. Trust me mate, the hard part's over. Finito. You'll never have to work again for starters."
"I never did before."
"Eldorado ... that makes things even better then."
"You're used to it, aren't you?"
"Fair point. What are we going to do about the 'lovers Grimm' though?" asked Martin.
"Nothing. Why complicate things? Once we've got the money I'll offer them a small share, maybe $90,000, and then we'll take off into the sunset. I don't think they'll alert the authorities, do you? It's not likely with their criminal record. They can do what they like with the cash. They could buy a farm, open a shop, become gambling addicts, fly home ... whatever, so long as they're not clinging onto our coat tails."
"Are you sure?"
"Yeah. I took one hell of a risk taking all that money out of 'Cym'. I don't need a murder charge hanging over me ..."
"Okay, deal."
"You're on."

§

A week or so after the 'Rosechain/Spoonface' incident Kathy was still in seven minds about Anthony's clumsy attempt at making a date. She'd already cancelled twice. Her first refusal was genuine, her father's birthday falling on the same day, but unfortunately, this level of honesty set a high standard for future communication and was never likely to be maintained. Especially not when he only gave her three days between queries. 'Not tonight Josephine, I'm having dinner with my aunt' was her favourite excuse. It was a blatant lie, not least because she didn't actually have an aunt. The sole redemption for her treacherous words lay in Anthony's continued harassment and dreary, clichéd nature. Not that she hadn't partially enjoyed the attention. That was all part of the deal. She'd assess her options, string him along a bit more, do whatever was necessary ... or so she thought. She didn't really know. She was on the sofa, thinking things over when Donna walked into the room.

"You watching anything?" she asked, pointing at the gray, dusty TV screen.

"Clearly not."

"Alright, you don't have to be like that!" Donna sulked, flopping beside her on the sofa.

"Like what?"

"Like, y'know, all defensive and superior."

"I'm sooooooo sorry Princess Donna. Next time I'll be sure to lay out a golden rug and bow politely," said Kathy in a twinkling, deceitful, voice.

"That's better," smiled Donna. She loved compliments, even sarcastic ones. It was one of the things Kathy found so endearing about her.

"I'll take it we're watching a Miss Bleak melodrama?"

"But of course, darling," replied Donna, leaning over to kiss her friend on the cheek. It was a warm feeling, lips against skin. She hadn't felt it in quite some time. Kathy smiled. Affection was fine, welcome even, but what she needed was that mixture of lust and passion that only a handsome man could supply.

"How's Anthony?" asked Donna.

"Don't ask."

"He's been bothering you again? God, he's keen! They usually get the message after ten rejections ..."

"Yeah, well, He won't leave me alone. I turn around and he's behind my shoulder. I go to dinner and he's perched on the next available seat. I go shopping and he's hovering near the bread counter ... I tell you, the

guy's a nightmare!"
"Yeah, right, come on. You love the attention, really," said Donna.
"No, I d ... alright, okay, maybe just a little," conceded Kathy.
"Thought as much. You're a real ice maiden y'know ... totally transparent."
"So I've heard," murmured Kathy. She didn't enjoy her friend's conclusion. Too many people were saying it and, very occasionally, the whispering millions were proved correct.

§

Lunchtime in the works cafeteria and for once, Kathy found herself sitting a safe distance from a certain Mr Anthony. Had Stephen Blobb not been sitting directly opposite her this may have signified a change in fortune. As it was, misery beckoned. Blobb, a failed novelist who liked to take his frustrations out on other writers, was rarely fun to be around. He hated chocolate and only smiled when he thought nobody was watching.
"Hello Kathy, heard the news?" he asked.
"No."
"Oh, right, I thought it might have reached your office by now. I suppose I'll have to spill the gravy myself then. You're going to love it.
There's good news and brilliant news!" cried Blobb, throwing his arms around as he spoke.
"You're leaving?"
"Eh?"
"Okay, what's the good news?" asked Kathy.
"I've been promoted" said Blobb.
"And the brilliant news?"
"I'm your new line manager."
"Fantastic," sighed Kathy, forcing a limp smile onto her otherwise horrified face.
"I thought you'd be pleased."

§

It was a blustery morning on board the Pelican Grange, perfect for kite flying but not so helpful when it came to the low fat outdoor breakfast Patricia Taylor had in mind. She liked to keep the boys happy.

"Patti, darling, something smells good!" said Ralph, clutching his hat to prevent it blowing away.

"You haven't tasted it yet," muttered Patricia, handing him a lightly buttered walnut crumpet. They were seated at a small round table on the upper deck, grinning at each other as Kevin slithered painfully up the steps. He would never have made a window cleaner.

"Big night, was it?" asked Ralph.

"Something like that. Fuck, my head kills. Don't know why ... I only had three glasses of wine and a weak Spanish lager," groaned Kevin.

"I hope you're hungry?" hissed Patricia.

"Come here," roared Kevin, suddenly embracing his far from ready wife in a sexualised bear hug. Ralph looked away in disgust.

"I haven't seen your friend, Martin, this morning," purred Patricia from somewhere beneath her husband's ample frame.

"You won't. Not today. He always does his bible recital on a Thursday. He's passionate about his religion y'know."

"Yeah ... when he wants to be," muttered Kevin.

"It must be nice to have something to believe in; must keep you focused. What do you think Kevvy?" asked Patricia, not having heard his comment.

"I reckon it's a load of bollocks," he replied.

"That's what he says about everything he refuses to understand," explained Patricia.

"It's a point of view," said Ralph nervously.

"Christianity is a philosophy based on fear; the fear of an invisible entity said to be present in us all precisely because He is actually present in none of us. Humanity flourishes by way of nurture, desire and conflict, rather than by adherence to the mythical rules of an unknown," growled Kevin, sipping his pineapple-laced vodka. He was happy now, basking in the sweet afterglow of an evening adventure. He didn't see the handgun poking through the railings. No one did.

§

Another night, another meeting, intolerable really; the way Steven commandeered his workers' free time to hold departmental reviews, but it was the way things had been going for a while. A national recession demanded action. Budgets had to be trimmed. It was, in truth, the only path to take when rival companies were folding like origami statues and intellectual curiosity was being obscured. That evening, to little general surprise, Steven had proposed a merger of the horror and light romance sections. No one really wanted it. They voted for it though, fearing for their jobs. Kathy was still reeling from the decision when she got home. Donna greeted her return with a dispassionate grunt, enthralled by Jasmine Bleak's latest adventure.

Kathy sat beside her on the sofa.

"How's it going?" she asked.

"Unlike you to be interested," replied Donna, all sulky. She was resting her head on a cushion and combing golden strands of hair with her nails.

"Yeah, well, I need the distraction tonight."

"Whatever ... if you must know there's been a murder at this weird country garage and, although local police are blaming Hells Angels, Jasmine thinks the quiet checkout girl might have done it. There's three other suspects too. A mad local vicar, a laundrette assistant who fancies her boss and a lion tamer called Cyril," said Donna in a tired voice.

"Oh."

"Complicated, eh?"

"Very. My guess is she falls in love with the vicar, who turns out to be sane after all, and arrests the checkout girl."

"What about the Hells Angels?"
"She probably killed them as well."
"Why would she do that?"
"Duh, because they witnessed the murder!" said Kathy.
"I disagree. I think the lion tamer's guilty. I think he accidentally killed the garage attendant while having a shootout with Hells Angels at the petrol pump."
"What's he got against the Hells Angels then?"
"I dunno ... maybe they tried to steal his lion," shrugged Donna.
"Sounds a bit mental, doesn't it ... stealing a lion?" teased Kathy. Donna gave her shut-up-and-watch-the-programme look at this so they both concentrated harder on the screen. In Jasmine's world she was visiting the checkout girl at closing time. She wore a stern black blouse, minus tie of course, and a determined expression on her pretty face.
"See, she's going to arrest her," whispered Kathy.
"Sssssssh," hissed Donna.

§

The checkout girl was beautiful; long dark, hair and a rich elegant figure. She didn't look happy to see Jasmine. Moving out from behind the counter she walked directly to the other woman, eyes blazing. Jasmine opened her mouth but instead of unleashing a venomous accusatory statement, she leaned forward and thrust her tongue between the counter assistant's lips, receiving an instant response. The garage girl held Jasmine's waist as they kissed. In the background a dramatic love song began playing.
"I didn't see that coming," confessed Kathy.
"Nor me," said Donna, feeling repelled yet fascinated at the same time. She struggled to suppress a shiver, acutely conscious of Kathy's soft, wet lips hanging scarcely an inch from her own.

§

Ralph smiled, stroking the champagne bottle, a Cheptomley 1976, marvellous vintage. He had good company and a sky blue sea to enjoy it with. Martin sat directly opposite, shaking with relief. They were lying on Javill Cyger beach, waves lapping at their sun scorched bodies with the sound of feeding parakeets leaping across from the trees surrounding them.

"This is the life," gabbled Martin, his voice sore with hunger and various other minor ailments.

"It very nearly wasn't," said Ralph.

"That's history now, man."

"True. History has its reasons. We didn't make those bad things happen, we just acted our parts in a play already written."

"You're being unusually philosophical ... considering we haven't even started on the champers yet," smiled Martin, feeling salt stinging his eyes and a sandfly slalom through the dying forest of his hair.

"Yeah, well, we weren't far away from the big black hole were we?"

"No. I think it's fair to say that the 'lovers Grimm have booked their tickets though."

"Not before time, either"

"Agreed ... sort of. I liked Pat," admitted Martin.

"Really? I couldn't see anything in her myself. She wore enough makeup to poison every fish in the amazon and she didn't exactly keep a tidy boat."

"She was quite funny though!"

"When?"

"I dunno ... at breakfast? I can't think of any particular example."

"Prob'ly 'cos there aren't any. You just can't resist a mother figure," said Ralph scathingly.

"I'm only human. She helped with the stress ..."

"What stress? It's worked out alright hasn't it? The Pelican Grange taken over by pirates, the Shipsmead fortune ours, and three weeks on this lovely desert island waiting for the boat to come in!" sighed

Ralph.
"Yeah ... but what are we going to eat?"
"We'll deal with that once we've had some champers. I can't search with a clear head."

§

The Anthony situation was still hanging over her, rearing its ugly head whenever she passed him in the corridor, so a touch of retail therapy couldn't have come at a better time. Kathy craved something more dynamic in her wardrobe, something to really turn heads on a night out. She didn't need to be loved. She needed to be lusted after. Maria was her usual shopping companion, her near flawless fashion instinct serving as an invaluable asset on many a Saturday morning superspree. She wasn't available though, so Donna's more enthusiastic, although less polished approach would have to do. Their first destination was Caroline's. This small, niche market chainstore was famous for stocking cheaper versions of the latest Moscow catwalk outfits. Today, however, things were different. Older, more conservative dresses lined the indigo shelves and Kathy was about to leave when Donna grabbed her arm.
"Hey, look at that!" she said excitedly, pointing at a shoulderless, black, PVC dress.
"I can't wear something like that ... it's practically a dominatrix uniform!" said Kathy, appalled.
"Come on ... it would look great on you!"
"No way."
"What if I try one on too?" pleaded the younger girl.
Kathy was ready to refuse again , embarrassed at the very idea of wearing such a garment, but then suddenly a switch flicked in her brain. 'Why not,' she thought, 'that dress will make me feel more powerful.'
"Go on then," she said. Donna smiled, her supple body almost bouncing as she picked two boxes from the rack. They entered the cloakroom, changing

hurriedly, anxious to put the new clothes on. Kathy finished first and stood examining herself in the round Gibraltan mirror. She looked spectacular. The black dress showed off her blonde hair superbly and the very high skirt did wonders for her legs.
"Wow! You look a-m-a-z-i-n-g," purred Donna, moving closer in the room's narrow, watery half light.
"So do you," said Kathy honestly. Donna's large vanilla white breasts were exposed to the nipples and her blonde hair shone like summer barley as it fell across her bare shoulders.
"I told you I'm a good judge," she breathed. Then, very slowly, she coiled her arms around Kathy's waist and pulled her close. Their breasts squeezed together. Kathy felt her throat go dry.
"I feel ... I don't know, really sexy," she confessed.
"You are really sexy," said Donna, arching her neck in slow motion and kissing Kathy gently on the lips. 'This is strange, this is wrong, this is wonderful' thought Kathy as their tongues met. She placed her jewelled hands on her friend's gorgeous curves and sucked her lips.

§

They'd finished the last fish-leaf pie and were still hungry. Martin had taken to chewing his shoelace. Ralph was in the process of biting a shard of tropical grass to its roots. Hope set with the sunset. Martin ran a bruised, shredded finger over his jutting ribcage, wondering how long it would take before he could use his prime biological armour as a potato peeler. Ralph grimaced. He was thinking of his home town. The crumbling, swollen factory, the boarded up shops, the ravaged schools, litter strewn playing fields, dreary weather, cheery pubs, glittering streets and running children. Perhaps it wasn't so terrible after all. He'd die here, a million miles away from it. Bitten by a bug. Or maybe not. Was that a woman swaying in the equatorial breeze?

§

"Hey, hey, Mart!" he cried.
"What?" moaned the latter.
"Look!" he said, indicating an undeniably female shape against a lifeless, silver-tinged background.
"Who is she?"
"The ghost of Brittany Murphy! Does it matter. The point is ... we're not alone" The two castaways watched, eyes on fire, as a tall bronzed goddess marched steadily in their direction. Her butterscotch hair was tied back in a loose ponytail, the faint hint of a bikini protecting her modesty yet lending a subtle splash of mauve to the tanned calves and smouldering stomach muscles. Ralph, his limbs guided by hypnosis, stood to greet her.
"Do you come here often?" he asked, idiotically.
"Nope. It's a special occasion," she called, her accent delightfully crisp.
"Are you a mermaid?" asked Martin. Helpless lust had dulled his senses. She was standing so close he could smell the salt on her ankles.
"I hope not," the woman said, laughing.
"Don't be stupid. You've come to save us, haven't you?" Suggested Ralph. He could picture the cruiseship's presence. A spacious marbleskinned vessel staffed by ex round-the-world yachtsmen and grand masseur;, it was clever of them to send a navigator from planet paradise.
"No. Sorry. Wrong girl. You'll have to disregard the lack of a uniform. It's too hot for that and, in any event, I may have to give chase if you
try and escape!"
"As if!" proclaimed Ralph.
"Good. Okay, well, I'm Jasmine Bleak and you're under arrest. The state has issued a warrant for murder, attempted murder, perjury, burglary, sexual deviance, fraud, money laundering, environmental terrorism, pet cruelty and ... ah, I can't be bothered reading the rest!"
She produced a rope in a flash, lasooing the

miscreants before they could argue.

§

Kevin gave Patricia a quarter of his shares. She deserved it. 'Cym' publishing was a major venture. It was crucial that no one-half of a power couple should attempt to monopolise their success.

THE BUBBLE PATTERN

Tamsin Marcus gazed at her reflection and smiled. Beyond the aught blonde hair, perfectly groomed eyelashes and shining, restless skin she could see an emerald highway, a dazzling, flowing path that led over the spikes of fear and on to a better world. No turning back now. She had her chariot at the ready, and her chaffeur on a ninty-five year shift.

§

It hadn't always been easy for her. As a child, growing up on the mean streets of Loughcamb Hamperley and Upper Thrithingham, she'd endured a much more difficult ride. Her parents were to blame. They'd shown little interest in expanding the family's 'mouse scale' advertising business and, as a result, Tamsin had felt hopelessly inferior in comparison to the other girls at Lucille de Vorgenshaw's internationally renowned finishing school. She could barely afford her own skiing lessons. It was a dreadful, situation to be in. Then, in 2018, Seesaw's bank had saved the day. Their near demise had caused Alexandria Cairo Seesaw, Tamsin's uncle, to seek recompense for his misfortune from the powers that be. He'd only wanted a few million. He wasn't greedy, more ... as Tamsin's mum pointed out ... a lobbyist trying to save people's jobs. And he got his just rewards. Twenty million of them. Uncle Alex was so enthralled by the unlikely loot that he pushed a third of the sum into Tamsin's lap then watched, with poorly concealed amusement, as she blew it all on space age beauty treatments, round-the-world trips and nights out on any town that would have her. Even Gook received a visit. They were dredging the merry humber for weeks afterwards ... until she realised she'd left her handbag in the taxi. A year later Tamsin's lifechanging fortune had shrunk to sixteen thousand pounds. At this point, sensing disaster, she'd sought financial advice.

"Stop whinging ... you've still got enough to bribe someone," A.C.S. had moaned.
So she had.

§

Kenneth Alterwhistle, a local hotel owner and recovering sun worshipper ticked all the boxes. He knew Tamsin's dad. He was useless at cricket. Best of all though, he spent most of his time running a health farm on the East coast of Scotland and the rest of it trying to remember how many managers his hotel actually employed. Sixteen, prior to Tamsin's offer. Based on a loose and constantly overlapping pyramid system, she'd paid off Alterwhistle's debts, bombarded him with compliments, and after a trial period which largely consisted of perfecting her makeup and memorising false qualifications, she'd sailed into the top job. Manageress-in-Chief. Envied by millions and with the whole universe's cultural sphere clinging to her marble-painted fingertips.

§

She eased her Lamborghini around Haylers Corner and scanned the view. It was a beautiful picture. The Schinnolpa Hotel hotel dominated Hapellswick Bay in the same way that a wedding cake would preside over tables supporting an otherwise regimental selection of buttered bread and stale buns. As to why the hotel had five towers rather than the customary four, and a drawbridge located on the third floor, nobody knew but it all added to the building's purple-bricked charm and general air of mystery. The location was similarly idyllic; forty miles from Brighton and twelve apiece from the ports of Marehaven and Trongly. People sometimes called the Schinnolpa 'Parsleyshire's glory' and over the decades it had become a magnet for upper class honeymooners, gratifyingly rich foreign businessmen and the fleeting ... often violent ... visits of international rock stars and ousted heads of state. She parked her car in the driveway, jingled keys in a self-important fashion and stepped inside. Kathy Sands was waiting for her. The other woman wore a razor-sharp business suit and a carefully constructed look of sheer devotion in her eyes.

"No more problems with the grocery deliveries this morning?" Asked Tamsin in a neutral voice.

"None at all. Mr Ralshley said he was delighted to accept our improved monthly offer which includes, of course, a guarantee of our ignoring not-completely-fresh veg so long as he accepts slightly less money overall," replied Kathy.

"Won't our guests notice?"

"They're not here for the breathtaking cuisine, Ma'am."

"Fine. Well done. That's another weight off my ... erm ... our shoulders," smiled Tamsin, secretly annoyed about her middle manager's success.

"A mere feather."

"What's on the agenda today, then?"

"You tell me," said Kathy, smiling sweetly, to show that she hadn't seen the malice behind her boss's smile.

"Well, I think the hardest task of the week's complete so you deserve a little time to celebrate. Other than that, there's the small matter of Neil Concubio, that irritating locksmith from the slums, and his bill. Oh, and could you do something about our registration archives ... there's been an enquiry by a Mr Jack Turnbull who apparently stayed here for three nights in the sixties and wants to know of his fellow guest's identities at the time."

"Another lost trainspotter?"

"He's very old school," said Tamsin.

"They all are," grinned Kathy, placing a stray eave of silky brown hair back into its correct position.

"If you're still seeing Dave then perhaps ..."

"Thanks, I am, you're an Angel," enthused the younger woman. She liked surprises. She patted her boss's arm before swaying purposefully into the next

room. Tamsin, meanwhile, had more pressing concerns. Needing a distraction, and aware that her afternoon was likely to be 'fully booked' she retired to her 1st floor office. It was a tastefully decorated arena. Minimalist design. A few bra-snapping novels on a papier mache bookcase while pink wallpaper, an empty desk and a 3D TV added colour and variety to her twin armchairs. She sank down on her favourite and reached for the remote control. Knock! Knock!
"Damn."
Her housekeeping general manager was loitering in the doorway.
"Would you like a biscuit?" he asked.
"No thanks. I'm watching my figure," she lied, trying not to look at his greasy black hair and scented, extended eyelashes.
"You seem perfectly normal to me," he drawled in a nasal voice.
"Goodbye, Ian," she said, shutting the door. Tamsin hated Ian Stanwell. He was a meticulously tidy but somewhat smarmy young man who used a cunning variety of emotional blackmail and nasty tricks to make his staff work more and more for less. He fiddled time sheets, tripled shifts and pleaded poverty. Ian, who claimed during his interview to be a married man, but who'd barely spoken to a woman outside his work, was obsessed with guns, swords, knives, harpoons, bombs and just about any other mechanised killing machine you might care to mention. He maintained he was 'protecting myself against weirdos and extremists'. He drove a stolen limousine and wore triangular sunglasses when off duty ... chiefly, it seemed, so he could leer at women without them knowing which way his pupils were facing. And, unfortunately, he was good at his job.

§

She held her breath before entering the archive room. It was a hideous place. Stuffy, smelly and dark. Congealing rock star's t-shirts – detained as 'payment' for trashed beds and wardrobes – ancient sheets, stained photographs and mangled electrical equipment reminded Kathy of a cupboard at the top of her grandparents' house. She wouldn't allow such things if she was in charge. No chance - they lowered the tone. Colour, modernity and neatness were her watchwords. Her five year plan. Her ever narrowing destiny. At twenty-six she had time on her side and, although lacking the natural elegance to be described as 'beautiful' she certainly qualified for a mid-table position in the league of very attractive people. Her looks had got her everywhere in life. From the silent admiration of male school acquaintances whose exam results she'd copied, to the frustrated graying businessmen who could no longer see any joy or reason in the fabric of their enterprises, Kathy cornered them all. And, oh, how she exploited them all. And, oh, how she exploited their self-fulfilling boredom. Ambitious and compelling, untroubled by guilt or fear, Kathy had cut her way into the services industry like a knife through soggy cardboard. With her long, brown hair always tied back, as if in readiness to spring out and strangle someone, she succeeded in hiding her ruthlessness beneath a veneer of innocent features and a limited armoury of self-deprecating humour. Now, having worked at the hotel for a year, she needed to raise her game. She wanted Yasmin's job.

§

"Where are you?" She sighed. A year was missing, 1963, the one Turnbull had requested. She'd have to start again. She ran her fingers along the dusty, orange-bound volumes, and just as she was about to give up a tatty stray revealed its presence in the narrow gap between 1984 and 1985.

"Gotcha!" she cried triumphantly. The book had clearly received more attention than its less battered stablemates, and she could see why. The guest list at the time of Jack Turnbull's stay was extraordinary.

He'd only stayed three nights. During that period, in early June 1963, Essemarlow James, Elvis Presley, John Lennon, Rick Malgorf and Alfred Hitchcock had all been resident at the hotel. Twenty 'unknowns' were also mentioned. The latter names, excepting one - Logarnna de Cyrilstone (because it was so odd) - escaped Kathy's notice, and she took great pleasure in pushing Jack's numbers into her mobile and waiting for the tearful response.

§

Ian had chosen his confidantes well. There could be few more promising candidates for a staff 'straightening' session than 'nailhead' Ned Langway ... six foot and eighteen stone of layered fat and muscle, Chandon Gattick ... a former prison drugs baron, and Mirabelle McNaught ... bitter, scarcely conscious, and willing to use underarm tactics should the going get tough. They were heading for the cellars where a rumour of clandestine gatherings amongst workers currently off duty had been passed on by Danver Ferrez.

"You know who the ringleader'll be," said Ian as they crept forward.

"McCluskey?" whispered Mirabelle.

"Bound to be ... long-haired student knob," muttered Ned scathingly. When they reached the utility room, underneath the main dining hall, a baby rabbit was seen scampering away in the flicker of faint light glowing beneath the door. Ian smiled. He nodded to his right and Ned, who'd loved crunchy noises since his first taste of Frosties, shattered the wood with one blow of his size fifteen boot. A cosy scene awaited them. A red and white checkered tablecloth covered a giant monopoly board. Cream, in a swan-shaped jug, strawberry jam, butter and high teas littered the cotton surface while, surrounding this invitation countryside extravagance, Calumn Strong, Mike Henry, John Griffin and the ringleader himself were huddled.

"What the f&*k's this McCluskey, a game of Chinese whispers?" Ian spoke with a menace he'd not have dared using had Ned not been breathing down his neck like a sea lion over a minnow it had decided to adopt.

"We're just having a chat ... about worker's rights," murmured McCluskey, knowing the game was up and sensing that lying could serve no purpose.

"Sounds like a pretty dull game to me," laughed Ian.

"Let's play caterpults," growled Ned, picking John up by his braces and tossing him aside. Mike was next. He made a half-hearted attempt to get away but was halted by Ian who tripped him up, and Gattick, who threw him across the room as though he was an empty milk carton. A loud splat followed. Ned put the boot in and Ian settled back to watch the real action, only raising his eyebrows when he saw Mirabelle draw a knife from the hem of her little citizen's blouse. She cut "I 'heart' you" into Mike's arm. Ian heaved an enormous sigh of relief. She might be mad and she might have had a chip on her shoulder the size of a mountain range, but she wasn't stupid. She'd covered their tracks.

§

The athletics stadium was on her way home. Dominique Shrutton usually managed a lap or ten before facing her family. It was a merciful release, a lovely escape after seven hours of being told what to do. She had 'Whip Me' written all over her face. Apparently it didn't matter who it was ... bosses, assistants, apprentices, work experience girls ... they'd all order her around and they'd never ask, or wonder, why she never tried to fight her corner. So she didn't tell them. It wasn't complicated anyway. The working day flew when you had a prize at the end of it.

"Alright, Min?" asked Arthur Davies, her fellow limbstretcher, as they crossed paths near the steeplechase pool. She looked up. His reflection

wobbled gracefully in the dirty, stagnant water.
"I think so. You?"
"Surviving. How's the hotel of horrors?"
"Oh, y'know ... nothing changes."
"Nah, no ... I s'pose not. I went to Roland's records this morning. Jackie Thomas's new album isn't out yet. They did have an amazing heavy jazz compilation out though; really good, a bit soulful. Dave let me listen to five songs on his headphone system," boasted Arthur.
"What's it called?" asked Dominique.
"I ... I ... dunno. Can't remember," admitted her semi-sparring partner.
"Oh."
"See y'later," he gushed, leaving for the canteen while there was still time. Dominique watched him go. Part of her wanted to gun after him but a larger part preferred to be left alone. Did he fancy her? She supposed he probably did. The red face, the nervous stammer, the majestic opening lines to conversations that never came close to fulfilling their true potential. He was a person trying to reach out for something. She sympathised and liked him though she hoped it wasn't her. She managed six more laps before sundown. She didn't want to stop. She was dancing in rhythm with the traffic and it took a wizened javelin carcass - disguised by darkness - to cajole her into abandoning the session.
"Nearly tripped me up," she said to the fossilised, empty main stand. It said nothing in reply. Half the seats were broken, faded or missing and the dressing rooms - in all their cramped, hostile glory - had been condemned. Instead, she made for a footpath opposite the long jump track; plastic on flagstones. A dull thud as she departed the stage.
"Hiya," said a male voice.
"Still here," murmured Dominique. Arthur had his back against the changing room wall. His right knee was raised, his worn spikes were scraping clouds of dust off the brickwork.
"Lost my keys," he admitted awkwardly.

"Again?" It was the second time in a week.
"Yeah. Well, sort of ... I threw them away ..."
"Why?"
"I'm thinking of giving it up. The running I mean. I ain't getting any better and, y'know, with the work and everything. I dunno whether its worth the hassle..."
"Everyone goes through a bad patch!"
"My cousin beat me at the four hundred metres yesterday."
"Not Bob?
"Yeah."
"Oh ...right, yeah. Look ... come on, be positive. He's ... he's probably on speed!"
"Are you calling my cousin a druggie?"
"No, no, no, totally no! I wouldn't dream of it. He's a great kid. Really cute. How ... how old is he?"
"Twelve," noted Arthur morosely.
"Yes, and so tall for his age!"
"S'what they say."
"Exactly. Don't give up Arthur. You're a natural runner, a proper athlete, and anyway, you're my friend."
"Cheers," he mumbled.
'Did he actually lose his keys or is he stalking me?' Wondered Dominique as she went to get changed.

§

"My God, what happened to you?" cried Tamsin. She opened her door to Graham McCluskey, her lover, mentor and best friend in the whole world. He didn't look well. A four inch gash, still gleaming with fresh blood, had been drawn across his face from nose to chin while a plump lump adorned his high and noble forehead.
"It was a gang, near the docks. I don't know why they picked on me."
"Oh no, Graham, not again ... how many of them where there this time? Did you call the police?" She threw her arms around his waist, doing her best to

kiss the pain away.
"I'd rather forget about it. Honestly. What would I tell them ... the truth? The truth is, it was pitch black. I couldn't see their faces and one of them hit me so hard I blacked out for a while. That must have been when they cut me ..."
"Cowards." She drew him closer. There was shouting in the flat upstairs and the sound of waves crashing on the shore as their lips fused together in a deep, passionate embrace.
"You're all I've got, you're all I've ever had," she moaned.
"And the hotel?" whispered Graham, breaking the spell.
"I hate the place. All those horrible bricks and beds, beds and bricks ... it's all so awful."
"Then why stay there?"
"It's what's expected of me, silly," sighed Tamsin.
Graham smiled. He'd always thought there'd be a rational reason for her behaviour, beyond the excuses of ego mixed with inherent greed, and now at last he was getting closer to the truth.

§

Ned had saved his finest muskets for musket-mad Ian, the intellectual. He loved Ian like the brother he'd never had; wanted to serve him above him all other people and all other things. Ian was his nation, not England - which had disregarded his presence from the moment he was born. Ian was his country, his seas and trees and broken countryside. It was nearly time to get up. Begin his magic formula routine. The dogs all needed to be fed so it was fortunate they were made of metal, all they needed was pedigree two-stroke every six weeks and the odd walk around a seedy warehouse on the edge of town. The metal was pure northern steel and Ned was proud to support his fellow workers, all victims just like him, instead of paying through the nose for some warped foreign cross-breed designed with nine legs, three brain cells and only half an ear.

§

Ian was a worker too, just a different kind of worker. He used his brain. He ploughed a wider furrow. Ned was happy to stand up for him in situations where Ian's verbal skills might prove inadequate, and occasionally necessary violence would be the end result. Like yesterday. McCluskey was a spymaster's whore, in the pay of North Korea according to Ian, and it was nearly time for him to receive his 'special warning'. Ned pondered over this as he got dressed. What did Ian have in mind? A sword to the throat? A poison attack? Another lively kicking? A little voice was singing at the back of his head. The voice expressed bewilderment at McCluskey's southern accent when he was supposed to hail from North East Cuba, surprise at his 'heavy denim' dress sense since he was said to be a 'native indian', and horror at the thought of beating him up again. He pushed such negative thoughts away. How could he contemplate disloyalty when Ian had done so much for him? He finished administering lotion to the hounds, kicked open his front door and dragged the mechanical marvels off on a tour of the local estate.

"Hello, Ned," said old Mrs Chamberlain, passing him at the corner of Mourguard road.

"Hello, love," he replied.

"Keeping well?"

"Always."

"Good," she smiled, hurrying past. She was always in a rush that woman. It was as though she ran a soup kitchen for seagulls. A middle-aged man, his red hair glowing against the darkening sky, was skipping past her, his cheeks pale, his eyes blinking nervously as they glanced in Ned's direction. It was John Griffin.

"Lovely day," remarked chirped Ned as they came face to face.

"Alright, mate," lisped John.

'That was rude,' thought Ned, watching his workmate

disappear behind the post office. 'Why the attitude?' Did John really think Ned wanted to crush his fingerbones?

§

It had been an exhausting day of nail varnishing, and Tamsin was gasping with relief as she slid open the doors to Schinnolpa 's best situated balcony, only to find Kathy already there.

"Hi," she said, coolly.

"Hello, what are you doing here?" said Tamsin, trying to keep the annoyance from her voice.

"Enjoying the fruits of my labour, as you suggested."

"How's the Turnbull problem going?"

"Fine. I found the names he was looking for. There were loads of celebrities staying here then but he was only interested in some guest I'd never heard of ..."

"Oh, who?"

"Logarnna de Cyrillstone?"

"Sounds unfamiliar. Great name though!"

"Yeah. Jack's trying to get in touch with him."

"Poor bloke," said Tamsin, causing Kathy to laugh as if it were the funniest thing she'd ever heard. Tamsin giggled with her. Despite herself she couldn't help admiring the other woman's professionalism, easy humour and goods looks; they made her own job so much more straightforward.

"I suppose I should be getting back." Kathy eased herself up from the chair and tried to squeeze past Tamsin and out through the door. She didn't quite succeed. The gap was tiny and, briefly, their bodies meshed as one, Tamsin's breasts heaving as they made contact with Kathy's.

"This is cosy," joked Kathy.

"Perhaps we need wider doorways," replied Tamsin a second later, once they'd prised their bodies apart.

§

There were sixteen lights in the lower staffroom (a space barely larger than most kitchens), and all were a product of their previous owner's fear of the dark. Not that Michael Hikstrigen was famous for his largesse. He'd been a cruel, vicious, miserly, manipulative man for the majority of his ninety-seven years and everyone, old and young alike, agreed that Alterwhistle's largely absent leadership was a vast improvement on the previous regime. Ned was sitting in Michael's kitchen. He'd completed his sweeping duties and decided to celebrate with a slab of strawberry cheesecake and a packet of lemon tarts. The glitzy chemicals were now sizzling, like barbecued fireworks across his tongue. He saw stars. He saw a dream-shaped gap in the future and a ribbon-shrouded elfin-temptress riding clear of the sinking, concrete sky.

"Sort it out Ned ... we ain't got time to gorge ourselves."

The cleaner spun around. It was Ian, veins bulging, arms moving in slow motion as they brought a rake crashing down onto Ned's back. The prongs hit their target. They scratched and tore and sculpted while their recipient, defiant to the last, refused to scream, rejected the temptation to display his agony as rust, blood and sweat dripped over the antiquated furniture.

"Sorry, boss," he said, sheepishly

"It's the man in twenty-four. He's a fucking journalist, the bastard, and to think I gave him his breakfast in bed on Monday morning. We've got to have his money, Ned, we deserve it more than he does."

"Don't worry, boss. I'll have him," croaked the helpless response.

"Good boy," smiled Ian.

§

A huge crowd thronged the beach that day. It was the biggest Jack had ever seen, and, although he didn't recognise any of them, he felt more at home than he had at any previous point in his twenty-one years. A unity of purpose. A ring of hope. The war was over and the coast was heaving with the masses, from Scilly Isles to Shetland Isles, from Margate to Marizion, on smooth sunny beaches and jagged, towering clifftops. Wherever there was light, moisture and watery English sunsets there would be love, peace, equality and freedom. No one could deny the people now. They'd died for an un-caring aristocracy, a haunted death-maze of slithering wretchedness, and they weren't going to be fooled again. A village girl with mud in her beautiful ginger hair took Jack's arm and led him gleefully towards the bonfire, away from fear. Then, in splashing peals, a bell was ringing and a man was beckoning him to come closer. The man cut a strange, otherworldy figure. He wore a perfectly tailored suit, a silver earpiece and a perfume which smelled like marbled poison.
"I'm not doing it!"

§

Jack had woken up. The neighbours were more reliable than most alarm clocks, and he was relieved not to be confronting the bloke in his dream. He didn't have the weapons anymore. He tumbled out of bed and hobbled across to the toaster of no return.
"Brown or white," he mumbled, eyeing the 'KICK OUT RACISM NOW' heading leering at him from the secluded comfort of a magazine He hesitated. The phone rang.
"Hello?" No answer. A clicking sound. Still no answer. He gave up. The Nokia priest smirked in the web of his whirring radiation lines while his morose minions crawled desperately along the hope-stained corridors

of their venerable suburban tombs. Eyes pleading. Shoulders primed to embrace the fear. Jack slapped some butter on a slice of wholemeal and lifted the crust to his lips. He thought about Logarnna de Cyrillstone. That night in the dining room. Stale chips sinking under a mayonnaise tide as Rick Malgorf revealed his regrets, ideas and loves to the boy in suede-street clothing; Logarnna blinking, secrets slowly filtering out. Jack sitting at the next table pretending to be interested in coffee granules. Was it really possible? Did the foremost intellect on the lounge-rock scene honestly not suspect he was being de-mystified?

§

He chewed hungrily at his snack. He could still see Rick, pink shoes glistening, scarf bobbling in the hurricane as he left Schinnolpa the next day. A lighter man. Logarnna watching from the adjoining table. A waiter armed to the teeth with celebratory wine. Jack was eating his full English in silence, wondering why Logarnna had risked exposure on such a puny target, why he'd faked journalistic credentials in the first place, and where, ultimately, his real ambitions lay. "CYRILLSTONE WINS ENGINEERING PRIZE" provided a clue. It also gave Jack an idea. He brushed the newspaper to one side and slipped a nicely-ironed duffelcoat onto his heavily perspiring back.

§

Tamsin had called Ian in for questioning, or, as certain people liked to call it, an informal chat. A clearing of the air. He'd sacked a third male porter in less than six months and eyebrows were quivering on the health farm. Alterwhistle was threatening a return.

"They simply weren't up to our standards. All of them tried hard, John especially, but I know how you won't accept anything less than the best. I couldn't let you

down," he said.
"But, surely, some of your finest workers have taken their time to develop?" she replied.
"I can tell though, it only takes a few days. The cracks soon show. The odd bit of sloppiness here, the odd tactless comment there ... and you know what they say about cracks. A few small ones can lead to a crevasse."
"Yes, and you know what they say about actors with big ties and small parts?"
"No," grunted Ian.
"They finish up blinding themselves with all the linen," noted Tamsin, quietly.
"I'll keep that in mind."
"I hope you will. Mr Alterwhistle's very keen on his healing projects and I wouldn't like to see him being dragged back into hotel management affairs. It doesn't suit him ..."
"True."
"So, you'll be good?" A reluctant nod indicated that Ian was, at least for now, willing to play the game.
"Thank you. I appreciate it. I've got a few things I need to be getting on with at the moment and, if you don't mind, there very much single person jobs ..."
"Understood," said Ian, clicking his heels before leaving the room.
"Phew," breathed Tamsin, as she reached for a copy of Daisy Longcliffe's latest. She was on chapter seven. The heroine, a tall, elegant woman from a remote country town, preparing to marry the man of her dreams. He, unfortunately, was a carpenter. It didn't matter though. A series of rich, gullible, benefactors were looming on the horizon and Tamsin sensed that a knight in shining steel was more than ready to state his case. She licked her fingers and turned the page.

§

A chocolate-encrusted shower curtain lay between Dominique and freedom. Custard yellow, with circling floral patterns and a scarlet edge, its immodest retro beauty had succumbed to a cruel mixture of Osherhausen flake bars, caramel creams and carob delights. She couldn't imagine what room 64's occupants had been up to. She didn't want to. They'd seemed like a lovely couple. She sighed, grabbed her brush, and began to scrub.

"You look exhausted," said Kathy, appearing suddenly in the doorway.

"I'm fine."

"Kinky were they?"

"I don't know," replied Dominique. She had no desire to speculate on Mr and Mrs Hempersham's possible sexual deviances with Kathy. They weren't friends. She tolerated, rather than respected her direct superior and made every effort to avoid her outside the necessary ritual of taking orders.

"Will you be long?"

"Ten minutes."

"Make it five. I need you to clean number twenty. It was Avril's job but she's useless that girl, always talking on her phone, always leaving stains under the sink. I wouldn't let her get away with it if I was in charge. It's Tamsin's fault. She's a soft touch."

"Oh," murmured Dominique. She'd heard the same speech a billion times. Kathy's rousing chorus. A call to arms. A manifesto of unambiguous ruthlessness which was designed, manufactured and sold in the crumbling temples of a disorientated semi-elite in the hope of maintaining tepid belief and vacuous practicality in the mortar of a system ripe for collapse.

"Well ... I won't hold you up," said Kathy, patting her assistant on the arm. Dominique shivered at her boss's touch. Ice-talons lingering on corporate clothing. Closing in. Twisting the jagged knife and then laughing that manic laugh, that bursting drum of madness, that orchestra in the theatre of sleeping elephants.

§

High above leafy Meddlestone, in the valley of the mortgage saints, Tamsin Bethany Marcus was picking at a stale drop-scone while pondering her next move. Greece or San Diego? Sun or sunshine?

Holiday dreamsdotcom was a modern marvel, a girl's best friend, and she wanted them to make the decision for her. Take some responsibility. Send a handsome man, in a star-pressed shirt, and a flying bus that wore its sophistication lightly. She stirred her coffee and studied the screen. Bright colors, bubble writing, and flashing pound signs. Money was no object. She'd grown tired of keeping a tight lid on hotel finances and had, instead, decided to favour a far more creative approach.

§

Her first dalliance involved shoes. She'd serenaded them at an exclusive shop on the high street and used her company card to gain possession. It was an entirely requited love affair. Passion and commitment on both sides. Tamsin, however, needed a new buzz. She abandoned her traditional tactic of buying Graham dodgy lefty books for his birthday and, to show she still cared, hurled a leopard fur sofa in his direction. He'd purred contentedly in gratitude. He'd sent her sweets. The lone cloud in Tamsin's golden sky was the fear that Alterwhistle may recover from his harmonised-lettuce delusion and demand a realistic share of what were, after all, his own profits. Stranger things had happened. Bankrupt pop-stars had failed to reform their scattered bands.

"Is everything okay?" asked a purple-skirted waitress as she drifted past.

"Perfect," smiled Tamsin. It was the kind of service she liked. People who respected her. People who were interested in her emotional and culinary requirements.

§

The Oar Seekers cafe was founded by Zokus Diphonma, an obscure religious sect, in 1793 and its latticed porches, carved hogs and genteel location always made her feel at home. She peered through the window. An elderly lady in a conical hat was locked in conversation with the vicar and, approaching Leyvre road, a scruffy schoolgirl had discarded her jumper letting her arms swing free. 'Me, ten years ago', thought Tamsin. Her phone rang.

"Hello?"

A male voice answered. Familiar, clipped, desperate tones.

"Hi, Kenneth here. I'm glad I caught you. How's my favourite manageress?"

"Terrific," sang Tamsin, presuming it was just another call about the Fen Gooey shortages.

"Jolly good. I ... er ... I'd love to say this is purely a social call but, alas, I have a compulsion to tell the truth. I trust it won't disturb you."

"What is it?" hissed Tamsin, already tiring of her alleged superior's verbal meanderings.

"Well, er, without wishing to appear ungrateful, and self pitying, and desolate, I'm in trouble. Virtually broke. Bottom's fallen out of the health farm market. I can't get government funding anymore, and as a result our clients have all upped javelins and gone A.W.O.L. I blame myself. The garden centre visualising meditation technique did nothing for my customers' health and I realise, now, that mending badgers slashed legs with bicycle puncture repair kits doesn't necessarily aid the vets, or animals, in their self-esteem issues. I'm an idiot," confessed Kenneth.

"No you're not, you're a brave innovator!" gushed Tamsin.

"Maybe."

"So, er, what will you do now?"

"Come home. It's definitely the sensible option. My accountant, Tony Fitzolomew, reckons I should be squeezing higher dividends out of the Schinnolpa and I'm inclined to agree. One can't allow a thriving business to go stale. You've done a brilliant job Kathy, an absolutely marvelous job, and it's time you received a helping hand ..."

"When were you thinking of dropping by?" said Tamsin.

"Tomorrow, ideally, and it's not a temporary visit. Tony's going to study the books, make suggestions, etc, etc, and, I suppose we'll take it from there," drawled Kenneth.

"Wonderful. I'll, er, I'll see you soon then?"

"You will indeed," growled the ominous reply.

"Goodbye."

"Nighty night. Enjoy your evening." Click. The phone was dead. Tamsin, though, sprang to life. She attacked her wardrobe with relish, hurling dress after dress after trouser-suit into a huge wicker laundry bask and guiding a dozen cotton scarves towards the car. She'd driven home from the restaurant in record time. Scared a gang of malingering rooks. She finished her packing, straightened her hair, and set sail for Parsley town.

§

The singer sucked savagely on a cough sweet as he surveyed his audience. They were the usual tepid, passion-free, crowd. Filling in the gaps. Trying to enrich their tragic lives by visiting an empty pub, seeing a has-been crooner, and boring their friends with the details at work the next day. He shook his head in despair. What to wail next? 'Geronimo Thundercase?' They wouldn't like it. He didn't care. He gazed at the wilting masses and patted his guitarist's knee.

"Great atmosphere." said Calumn.

"He's still got it," added Mike.

"Yeah, even so, it's hardly an appropriate venue for a trade union meeting," murmured John, doubtfully. "Perhaps ... they serve us, though, don't they? That's

more than you can say for The Solicitors Arms, or Devs Cafe or Millies Diner or The Lost Shepherd or Cayston Country par ..."
"Alright, alright, I get the picture," hissed John.
"And I love the paintings."
"Lucky you."
"Where's Graham? He's an hour late!" noted Mike.

§

They were sitting at a round, smokey, table near the bar. A safe distance away from Malgorf's microphone. A trio of slightly wooden looking couples were the only other customers present and the barman, a spindly man worn by nervous spectacles, had rejected service duties in favour of the Meddlestone form guide. He usually won. He'd trained as a greyhound psychologist.

§

"I don't think he's coming," moaned John.
"This place was his idea."
"I love the smoke. Reminds me of the good ol' days. D'ye remember Thursdays at the Iyver? Every night was bonfire night. Mad Maizie dancing through the mist, Kenny doing his stuff, and Cello Cowcher screaming like a wounded fighter jet as insults whizzed around his ear."
"Have you seen Cello lately?"
"Nah. Graham says he moved away."
"It's what I should've done,"said John, sadly.
"Don't talk soft."
"It's her, innit?" murmured Mike.
"Eh?"
"Tamsin. She's with him. She must be."
"No way mate. They're over. He went round her place three weeks ago and broke it off ... said the whole thing was stressing him out," claimed Calumn, nodding to Malgorf's mawkish beat as he spoke.
The crowds were thinning. Two couples had left and

the third was clearly in no mood for an encore.
"Hello ... look what the rain washed in," cried Mike. A chill went down John's spine; it wore ragged, fancy-dress surplus clothes, denim shoes and a purple-velvet cap which was tilting, horribly, to the wrong side.
"I'm not in the mood," said John.
"I didn't know you drank in here," remarked Calumn.
"There's always a first time," replied Ned, laying his pint down on the table. Mike shivered from head to toenail. He could smell Ned's breath, the wine, and rum, and whiskey, and he hoped, if there was a punch-up, that it would be over fairly soon.
"What's your poison," asked Calumn.
"Ian Stanwell."
"No, I mean ..."
"I know what you mean. And I know what I mean. We've got to do something. He's changed my shift pattern, the bastard, and he's threatening to sack the computer for breaching in-house dress rules."
"You're joking?"
"Do I look like I am?"
"No." Calumn shrugged. His colleague had disconcerting, earnest eyes, eyelids shaped by violent passions, and he was the type of person who normally gyrated his own arms at merest mention of dishonesty.
"Yeah ... so I'm, er, with you. I want to do my bit. Join the union and stuff, organise fundraisers ..."
Mike dropped his glass. John, imprisoned by doubt, tried to re-wind his twenty-four hour memory. Amazingly it produced the same results. A nerveless statement of intent. A crushing, brave endorsement of the struggle against tyranny, apathy, greed, hesitation and despair.
"Are you sure?"
"Yes."
"Okay, well ... we, we should drink to it!" proclaimed Calumn.
"Your round," said Mike.
"No, no, I'll do the honours," insisted John.

He needed an excuse. He was still frightened of Ned, and all the political u-turns in the solar system weren't going to alter this grubby, wholesome little fact.
"I'm sorry," said Ned after John had gone.
"What for?"
"The beatings."
"Oh ... yeah ... them."
"They didn't hurt," laughed Mike.
"No?"
"I dunno. I ... tell me if I'm wrong, but I sort of got the feeling your heart was never in it. Hurting us, I mean. Making us suffer."
"I wanted to help Ian. Nothing else mattered. If that involved kicking heads then I'd make myself enjoy it."
"Right, er, so, why the massive re-branding exercise?"
"I told you. Ian's losing the plot. I was a brother and a protector to him, yet he treated me like a performing rhinoceros at a country zoo. Or worse. I'm so stupid. It's my fault. If Jack Turnbull hadn't told me about Alterwhistle I'd prob'ly still be tongueing Ian's trainers now."
"Jack who?"
"Turnbull. He taught me to stand up for myself. To be truthful. To believe my eyes,and my ears, and not to let any symbols distract me. He's a wise man," replied Ned,rolling his arms to illustrate the point.
"He sounds it," agreed Mike.
"We should organise a strike," said Calumn.
"Isn't that a bit extreme?"
"How can it be? The situation's desperate. Tamsin's spending all our profits on her aristocratic illusions, half the staff are on minimum wage, and Alterwhistle's so absent he makes King Richard the first look like a sitting minister. It's a superb opportunity."
"Hear, hear!" roared John, stepping into the limelight with a massive grin on his face and a brace of drinks wedged under the palms of each hand.

§

The curtains were drawn when Tamsin arrived. She left her car on double yellow lines before climbing the steps, applying some cherry lipstick, and undoing the top three buttons on her blouse. Then she rang the bell.

"Babe ... hi," purred Graham, leaning down to kiss her.

"I'm leaving town," she said.

"What?"

"I can't take it anymore. That place is driving me mad. I've worked five eighteen hour days this week, for no extra reward, and there's a taxi-load of Epitomian bankers coming next week. What a nightmare. I don't speak the language, Kathy doesn't speak the language, and they're refusing to communicate in ours. It's ridiculous."

"Don't be silly. You ..."

"I've made my decision. I just thought I'd let you know."

"Come inside. We can talk things through. I've got a strawberry flan in the oven and a bottle of champaigne that won't drink itself on the sideboard."

"Goodbye," whispered Tamsin, turning away. His eyes followed her. They demanded proof. They saw a slim, graceful woman descend a flight of marble stairs and they blinked in a rush of frenzied terror as she stopped beside the outline of a car door.

"Wait!" he yelled.

"No time."

"Where are you going?"

"Cumbria. My auntie owns a little cottage ..."

"I'm coming with you!" he shouted. He felt alive. His words bounced off the brickwork and danced, merrily, along the empty suburban street.

§

Kenneth Alterwhistle hobbled back to the Schinnolpa a beaten man. He'd endured a tortuous twelve hour train journey, during which every station en-route had reminded him of an ex-customer who'd hastened his health farm's demise. The Darlington room wrecker. The Doncaster thief. Peterborough health and safety guru. All guilty. All scraps of rotten fat in the flesh market of human survival. He was so immersed in his problems that he missed a new sign which decorated and dominated the end of Schinnolpa driveway. It would prove to be a fateful error.

PROPERTY OF THE BUBBLE PATTERN UNION.

CHOKEENAW HOUSE.

I was born long after the revolution, in a small village on the Parselyshire-Sussex border. I was an exceptionally gifted child. I could add, subtract, divide and rule before my third birthday and, at age seven I composed a seductive melody that swept the honours at a prestigious local fishing contest. I've still got the press cuttings; a self absorbed child grinning mischievously from behind a canvas shield. Completely unafraid.

§

My parents were intent on sending me to boarding school. They maintained that despite being almost unaffordable it would 'pay dividends in the long run'. Like hell. They just didn't want to burden themselves with my potential. Great things were being predicted and, should the future turn out to be not as rosy as planned, they'd at least have a ready scapegoat. Their cynical tactic worked. St Ellemon's academy was a disaster. One of England's six remaining fee-paying schools, propped up by minority culture grants and backroom deals, it delivered a bizarre curriculum based on the obscure principles of six elderly scientologists, two bitter ex-sheikhs and a mug manufacturer called Grommick. The schedule was exhausting. Eight hours of compulsory religious education per day, plus a nominal fifty minute stab at English, Physics, Languages and kiln-firing, all in one lesson. In the evening interested parties were allowed, although not encouraged, to attend a Maths class. I declined. I love mathematics in all its wondrous forms but the teacher, a Mr. Brenton Pipe, terrified me, and anyway seven p.m. was smoking hour.

§

I received a one year sentence at St Ellemon's. In that time I lost all interest in study, and, by many accounts, had developed into an awkward, obnoxious, unstable youth. I threw paint pots at pigeons. I shoplifted. I became so frightened of girls I took three mile detours to avoid them in the street. I was a social disaster. My worried parents enrolled me in the nearest community school in a desperate attempt to save the situation and, for a while, I flourished. I was back in the social whirl, enjoying my maths and befriending twelve heavyweights like Ian Duke, Barry Simpson, Daisy Kite and Kevin McEwan. We formed a gang; did everything together. Ian's father, Stuart, was the mayor of Scorchers Hill. At that time, and during one long balmy summer, we played football, cricket and table tennis in his super-sized garden then swam in the river every evening, inventing countless board games. We also made a short film about purple squirrels. Bollywood expressed an interest. The Parselyshire Gazette ran a dozen or so favourable reviews, then in late September Barry announced he was leaving town. We couldn't believe it. The Simpson family had held Scorchers Hill social fabric together for hundreds of years, ringing bells, conducting choirs, teaching infants etc, etc and now, NOW they were abandoning ship; letting us down. Barry's mum had landed a major research job at the internationally renowned Purple Squirrel Preservation Institute in Canada. The whole family, including four cousins and a great grandma, were upping sticks.

§

Things were never the same after that. None of us could match Barry's subtlety, strength or charisma, so the gang simply fizzled away. I concentrated on studying, trying to catch up. I'd acquired, quite miraculously, a girlfriend - Naomi Wallis. She'd proved invaluable, both as a lover and a shoulder to weep on throughout the crushing turmoil of year thirteen exams. We were like the gang in miniature, playing two roles each. Barry of course was irreplaceable, but she linked Daisy's generous practicality to Kevin's dreaminess in a seamless fit. I had a little difficulty mastering my own and Ian's roles. We'd re-invented the old gang. Our results arrived in August and, despite being lower-than-expected, I was able to join Naomi in gaining a place at the University of Halven, in Brellandshire. That's where the real story begins.

§

We'd been together at the college for two months but were already drifting apart. Inevitable, I s'pose. A summer of love, hope and desire had been replaced by an autumn of the same, except - the things I loved, hoped for and desired had all changed. Let's start with the love. This intense feeling, once focused exclusively on Naomi, now seemed spread in a thousand different directions. The trouble was, Halven University had hundreds of female students in my age range and, after my initial, slightly fabricated shyness had worn away, I soon discovered most of them were more interesting than Naomi. This, in many ways, had been a horrible discovery. I'd worshipped her early in our relationship but now I hated the ambivalence I felt. It cheapened us, threw a dark blanket of pointlessness over the recent past. So, before I pollute the page with more revelations of self-disgust, let's move on to hope.

§

I honestly don't know what I was hoping for when the course began. It was certainly an improvement on maths and I'd heard enthusiastic proclamations from numerous parties on the rewards of forging a career in the oil industry; not that I cared. A job would always be available for me in Auntie Jaqueline's weaving business, but it was rocks rather than dead plants which inspired my fantasies. I loved their cold, hard, textures, their searing, odourless 'otherness', their eternal souls. Away from all this I saw the college as a way of postponing work's grim embrace; discovering unique cocktails, eating French breakfasts and meeting people from exotic faraway locations, like Sutton, Sunderland and Stranraer. I wasn't disappointed. On a first aid course in October, I met a boy with a Rutland accent. The library turned out to be a haven beyond my wildest dreams, vastly superior to the mean little collection of dust-pamphlets accumulated by generations of tight-fisted Scorchers Hill headmasters. I spent countless hours within its walls keeping the spiders company, foraging amongst the ruins. I had, for several years, possessed a reasonable knowledge of Parsleyshire's many and varied rock formations, but it was only the access to Medistia's Guide to Messianic Landscapes that enabled me to build the foundation for specialising.

§

As it happened, Mrs Colldey, the main lecturer, believed Medistia to be a lunatic, citing his belief in having lived through most of the Jurassic Age as evidence, but I disavowed such hang-ups. I remained committed to the cause. I needed a passionate guide. My classmates, meanwhile, were a highly irregular bunch. There was Millkie Cillsigen - son of a Marlbroske comb manufacturer, Miranda Dryllton - a junior ice dancing champion, and a tall, beautiful, golden-haired girl called Sarah Ketcherling. Sarah was blind. She didn't wear her condition lightly. At first I was scornful of what I perceived to be a self imposed, self defeating victim status. I was jealous of Miranda's patience and ability to describe the visual world to her friends. I tried, and failed, to hide my feelings. They DID matter. Millkie didn't hang around with us. He had a job outside college so it was usually me, Sarah and Miranda who socialised. I was wrong about Sarah. Once I'd got to know her I realised that surliness was her front, a shallow defensive mask, and that she really was a very funny, sympathetic, courageous person. A girl who paid her way. She helped more people just by listening to their problems than she received in return. Her kind face and sharp brain charmed students and professors alike. I was amazed she wanted to spend any time with me. We charted concert halls, painted fish stocks and went potholing. The only downside to our friendship was that Miranda began to feel left out, creating a friction, a tension between us I was never able to fully resolve. One afternoon, I think it was early November, Sarah and I were walking beside the river Whendron. We'd made slow progress. The Sunday lunch of stale ryebread, wagon wheels and rotten gravy wasn't helping and I could feel my stomach groaning as we sloped along on the crackling winter frost. Sarah was on my left, away from the edge, her arm in mine. She snuggled close. I smiled. Suddenly, breaking into our mutual peace zone, I heard a strange rasping noise on the path behind us. I turned my head. Nothing there. Sarah swayed slightly; the slightest shock could cause her great distress, and I had to catch her waist to stop her from waltzing into a spikily defended wooden fence.

"What is it, Melvin?" she whispered.

"Only a water pigeon. Nothing to worry about," I replied. It seemed a reasonable explanation. The birds are known for their genius in the art of camouflage and possess an intelligence vastly superior to their city slicker cousins.

"What does it look like?"

"Oh, y'know, the same as a normal pigeon, odd, silly and a bit vague. Purply-reddish feathers with little streaks of white here and there ..." I said uneasily. The noise grew louder.

"Liar. You told me they were green and white."

"Aah, but that was in a different light; a summery haze. Background is a crucial factor when it comes to birdwatching," I explained.

"You can't see anything there at all, can you?" she

hissed after a few seconds.
"Well, I definitely saw something move. The fact it didn't make any noise does, possibly, suggest a water pigeon." Sarah laughed.
"Come on! That's like eating a really horrible slice of onion pie and presuming Lisa Perronime can't cook," she said, flexing her vocal muscles in mock outrage.
"How do you know Lisa Perronime can't cook? Her mother was the finest caterer in Mulgatewood," I protested, trying to ignore the eerie chorus.
"Exactly. Her mum was a brilliant chef so she'd hardly have let anyone else near the kitchen, would she?"
"Yeah, well, I don't see how that follows. Most people who are good at a particular activity like to pass the skill on ... anyway, on a less appetising note, don't you think Miranda's virtually the spitting image of Mrs Perronime?"

§

Looking back, it was a stupid comment to make. Unnecessary. Miranda and I hadn't been getting on and I suppose this was a clumsy attempt to prove how much I admired the girl who was showing me so much hostility as a means to appear a better person in Sarah's eyes. Lisa Perronime was the most beautiful woman on British television.
"We should invite her to the cinema tomorrow," said Sarah, quietly.
"Who, Lisa Perronime?"
"No,Miranda, you idiot."
"Oh, right, yeah. She'd love a film about the civil wars of ancient Mesopotamia."
"I don't think she's very happy, Melv."
"Who wants to be happy. It destroys rational thought," I said, with a flippancy so ill-disguised that even the jackdaws laughed.

§

The following evening I arrived at Clobbermead cinema dishevelled and prodigiously weary. I'd run all the way. The seven mile dash had been undertaken as a challenge to Christian Mellgo's status as college long distance champion. I'd regretted my impetuosity from the start, losing sight of Mellgo near the hospital and almost collapsing outside Leycombe's garage. Twelve bemused onlookers witnessed my final, humiliating, capitulation. I'd grinned ruefully and staggered on. At the cinema, bruised, broken and dejected, I made strenuous efforts to haul my appearance back to the sunny uplands of respectability. I threw water all over my face. I straightened my shoulders. Still no sign of Sarah. Her absence brought Naomi's innocent cheerful, features to mind. I hadn't seen them for a long time.

§

We'd gone to see a film at Clobbermead on, what I now presumed, was the occasion of our last date. There wasn't much on, it being a wednesday evening, and we'd had to settle for 'NM 864-216, a Clostenwood radio odyssey', as the source of our entertainment. No wonder we'd split. There were only four other people in the audience, two film reviewers and elderly twins on the front row who kept replying to everything the actors were saying or doing. Naomi found this amusing, a diversion from the film's murderous grandiosity, but I was becoming absorbed in the picture and, according to Naomi's post-midnight evidence, I spent half-an-hour tutting in dismay at the twins' manic disruptiveness.
"You're getting really pompous and boring, Melv," she moaned after the film. Oh, so I was pompous and boring! How would she have felt if the strange brothers had prevented her hearing the all important tail end of Cappillon wood? Far from elated, I'd imagine.

§

Sarah's arrival was becoming more unlikely by the second. She'd already passed the forty-minutes-late-barrier, and the last stragglers were, as I watched, bundling inside the revolving doors in a feeble attempt to get a ticket before the box office girl grew tired of waiting and wandered off to the bar. I could guess what had happened. Sarah would have contacted Miranda and asked her to the film, mentioning my name in passing and trying to put a positive slant on the director's previous cinematic disasters. Miranda might scream, sigh, or shout gratefully in response. She'd play the martyr. She'd say that she didn't care what was showing because she just wanted to 'go out for a change'. This flimsy statement would arouse Sarah's sympathy, paving the way for an understanding reaction the next day when Miranda called say to say she was feeling unwell, wouldn't be going out for a while and 'could you come round tonight and keep me company ..? There's chocolates in the fridge and souffle in the oven.'

§

I took my frustration out on a lamp post. Inevitably, I came off worse. Time to go. If my explanation wasn't correct, then, well, it was close enough. I left the cinema concourse and walked along Bellowing road towards the town boundary. I didn't want to go home, nor was I particularly desperate for a drink, having consumed several glasses of wine before coming out, so a gentle stroll struck me as the perfect solution. Blackberries were sprouting on bushes above the paving slabs and there was a faint chill in the evening air, causing people to walk slightly faster than they had done in recent weeks. Or maybe the temperature was irrelevant. Perhaps the whole town was participating in a secret walking race which only I hadn't entered for. Oh well, when has a surprise winner ever done the world any harm?

§

A smashed-up telephone box marked the point where urban sprawl met rural obscurity. Fields, trees and shrubs lined the route ahead and, dazzled by their leafy 'otherness' I decided to turn back. I hate the countryside. It reminds me of boarding school. I spun round, about to retrace my steps when a young woman emerged from a badly overgrown nearby footpath. Her face was streaked with thorn scratches and dirty tears. She stumbled past me without saying a word and then, in ridiculous slow motion, caught her toe on a root and sprawled face down in the dying autumn mud.

"Are you okay?"I asked. She clambered to her feet. "Don't go down that path, whatever you do. It's not safe. It's poison. Go anywhere in the universe but don't go down that fucking path!" she shrieked, racing away. Curious. The bridle didn't look especially exciting. It was little more than a tangled opening in a hedgerow. Had I known the consequences I probably would have frozen on the spot and ceased to function as a human being. At the time, however, it wasn't a wildly difficult choice to make. The girl was clearly a paranoid delusionist, or something of that kind. I'd no desire to immerse myself in one of those lives after what had happened with Mark Kellstone. They were still unpicking his brain with chopsticks in a Zooscan hospital.

§

So, footpath it was. Or should I say, the footpath it wasn't. Years of neglect had allowed signposts to tumble and bequeathed a thousand varieties of weed space in which to regain the control which had originally been theirs. I stepped forward. I felt spikes against my skin. Broken brambles were the only recognisable guide to its route as the trackway led me along the edge of an elegant meadow, underneath some weary looking poplar trees, and down into a rough area of withered scrubland. Rough terraces cut across a gentle slope. They resembled a poor man's grand stairway to the three-stone house clinging, modestly, to the valley side. Blue lighting flickered in one of the windows, creating a far from welcoming picture, but everything else was shrouded in darkness, curtains drawn and rooms devoid of life. The building itself was a neat, modern affair. Chocolate-brown bricks formed the walls and a vast adjoining garage almost made up for the lack of chimneys. Six plainly large windows were situated at the wing of each floor, crowding out their narrower companions, while several fussy little balconies poked aimlessly out from the brickwork, as though trying to avoid the indignity of being stamped upon by human feet. Strolling over to the front door I reached for a cold, plastic handle but, at the same moment, my target swung free and a balaclava-wearing person, with no arms and a single leg, hobbled into view carrying a sharpened length of wood with a bloody, female head impaled upon it.

I screamed.

§

"I take it you're next, then?" growled a voice from beyond the wool. Relief shot through me like flint arrowheads. I recognised the accent.

"It's Don Litchen, isn't it?" I said, casually.

"And I suppose you must be Melvyn Wolgersom," replied Halven's most famous medical student as he revealed his face to the masses.

"Live autopsy of a hare, wasn't it?" I sneered, in reference to the video Don had made a year ago during a dutifully dreary summer. It had defied all expectations and reached the top of Portugal's DVD chart.

"A stoat, actually," he murmured.

"Stoats, horses, elephants, otters ... they're all the

same thing really. Who's the girls that you frightened?"
"Carla Frollix. She's guardian of this establishment. Nothing can happen without her written approval."
"May I ask if I'm allowed to come in?" I ventured.
"Carla wants to know your reason for wanting to enter this place," said the other.
"Nosiness ... and the fact that it doesn't seem quite, real." I answered honestly, wondering when or if Don was going to end the Carla pretense.
"She asks if you're an officially sanctioned reality inspector?"
"No, only a curious bystander."
That did it. Without saying another word he grabbed me by the arm and beckoned me inside the splendidly decorated hazelnut doorway. A vague, chocolatey smell tickled my senses as Litchen, eyes glowing, led me on a whistlestop tour. The building was a palace. Each floor had five rooms of marginally differing sizes, their walls adorned in a light 'crescendo pink' hue and the odd pastel painting which could have been of almost any landscape in the world. Carpets were conspicuous by their absence and, in the traditional Solifidian rural style, a small heavily matted rug lay in middle of the floor in every room. Best of all though, was the library. A line of bookshelves held most of the communist classics, from Marx and Engels through to Sempill, Gostanyia and Dezarbin, while above the main fireplace stood a beautifully manicured sixteen hour clock, hauling forth memories of the Groumarsh era when Brellandshire's shorter days gave it the longest life expectancy on planet earth. "Come to Brelle, live forever, and be a plastics machine operator," ran the surprisingly effective advertisements in continental copies of TIFORSIX magazine.

§

"Well, what do you think?" asked Don, grandly.
"Magnificent. It's like time travel without the fear."

I sighed, caressing the upholstery.
"And you've not even seen the romantic room yet," continued my new companion, laughing as he led me down some marble stairs and into a basement littered with worn out candle holders and childrens' toys without any limbs. On each wall hung green paintings of a lopsided urban world where gigantic mutant woodworms presided over steadily sinking, reinforced streets held up only by ropes, chains, enslaved coltus birds and dynamistic traffic holders. I was THERE now, part of the imagined chaos and drained of any desire for a return to the rivers of confusion that are paradise for most first year students.
"We could live here y'know," said Don. There didn't seem any reason not to believe him.

§

The next day found us waiting patiently in the Collett Road housing office. The man in front kept coughing. He was totally inebriated and, surely, a prime candidate for throwing back onto the street. But instead, as further evidence of appearances being deceptive, he separated his lips and revealed his true identity as a witty, sophisticated raconteur with the irritating ability of proving able to throw in a humorous and irreverent comment at exactly the right moment. Don attacked him with a barrage of jealous glances. I feigned indifference. When our turn came we were both in state of heightened fury. I could scarcely breathe and Don was growling, hissing, and snarling at the pens before making a dramatic late recovery. This saved us. I was left to sit and admire while he hypnotised the accommodation officer with a carefully researched routine.
"As far as I can gather the building's been empty for nearly a year and serving no useful purpose," he was pompously declaring, playing up to the tiny audience. "It's certainly possible that the Fosserlerns could have gone abroad, though I don't believe for a

second ..."
"Precisely, it's not just possible, it's almost certain. Don't you remember how old Jim Fosserlen always used to say that Uruguay was the only country for a fisherman's son? That's your answer. They've gone to South America." The housing guru lowered his eyebrows. He wasn't in the mood for arguing. He rummaged absentmindedly, through a sheaf of yellowing papers then slapped a brace of items on the desk.
"There's no record of Fosserlen's departure here. His tenancy registration agreement is, I admit, a little overdue b ..."
"Couldn't we at least join a waiting list for potential occupiers?" continued Don boisterously, his voice bouncing me back to life.
"Well, actually, no you can't! The house has been withdrawn, it isn't on any lists," said the officer, focusing intently on a cactus dying noiselessly on his windowsill.
"Withdrawn? How can it be withdrawn?" spluttered Don.
"Quite easily. It seems the Mr Fosserlen was so keen on no one else inheriting the house that he concocted a story about the foundations having been raised above an old, underground tinsel factory, the ceilings of which are likely to cave in without the slightest warning. He has, effectively, condemned the place amongst our local community."
"Meaning?" I whispered.
"As far as I'm concerned, and I'm sure there'll be no objection from my superior, you can move in tomorrow ... with one condition."
"What is it," snapped Don.
"That you get some more housemates. Chokeenaw is a pretty substantial residence and local council guidelines state that you'll require a good five names on the list. I can put false names on the form for now, I'm sure nobody will notice, but it can't be an ongoing situation. Understand?"
"No problem. There's loads of people who can't wait

to escape the halls," promised Don.

§

Katherine Greenwold, a nervous blond mathematics student, was our first signing and by the Sunday every bedroom was filled. I liked Katherine. She sang in the town choir and didn't complain when we failed to clean the cutlery properly. The final 'rails on the track' arrived an hour later. Paul Gilbert was a painfully neat architecture student who had once played teddy bears' football with Don's cousin, an ideal qualification apparently, and Sam McQuade ... occasional economics student and terminal gambler, just seemed to drift into the reckoning without any decisions having to be made.
'If only I could've designed something like this,' Paul had said, while me and Katherine were trying to talk Sam's pet giraffe into crossing the threshold.
"It's lucky you didn't. The college would probably have given you a lifetime ban," replied Don. His words fell on deaf ears. Paul's eyes were ablaze with the sordid magnificence of it all and he watched, mesmerised, as Sam began to regain control of his lift-shaft-necked companion.
"Do giraffes eat meat? I've still got a few tins of cat food left," asked Mirabelle Dustington, busy helping Katherine unpack. Don laughed and shook his head.
"Don't be silly," scowled Sam.
"Yes or no?"
"Nein. Why d'you think they have such long necks? It's not 'cos they like the view, it's because they need them to reach fruit on very high trees."
"Oh, right, yeah ..."
"Fat lot of use your one having a neck though. He only eats cabbage soup and ground peppers, the poor ol' boy," sneered Don.

§

In the evening we all sat on the logs decorating Chokeenaw's garden, and enjoyed a delicious meal of roasted vegetables, fried breads, honey-coated pasta and chocolate gateau. Sam did most of the cooking. He'd grown up as the oldest child in a large family and was accustomed to the star role.
"I don't think you did ANYTHING. I reckon you just said some kind of spell to make everything appear," said Paul, swaying slightly as he drained the last of a whiskey and cola.
"You've discovered my secret, you devil," answered Sam.
"Well, I simply couldn't eat another thing!" said Katherine, slipping a seventh slice of gateau between her lips. I was sitting on a rope swing with a television aerial in my hand. I'd found the perfect signal. I felt content, almost happy, and the early days of term were a million miles from my thoughts.

§

The next day we all woke up in various corners of the garden. It was a pitiful scene, bodies everywhere. Mirabelle and Sam were lying together under the table. I was careful not to wake them as I crept towards the house. I craved food. I negotiated the yellow corridor and let my instincts take control. The kitchen looked like a brush had hit it! There wasn't a stain or poorly angled cup anywhere; the crude smell of cheap disinfectant hung remorselessly in the air. I'd entered a domestic war zone. While my skin began peeling in response to the assault I was somewhat surprised to see Naomi emerge from the wilderness of our front room and kneel elegantly before the unlit open fire.
"Imoan! What are you doing here?" I asked, saying her name backwards in a way I'd fondly regarded as affectionate, but which was probably quite irritating.
"I just popped over to see if you were still pompous

and boring," she said, smiling.
"And?"
"I don't think that really needs an answer, do you?" she sang, nodding at the carefully scrubbed wallpaper and layers of meticulously labeled cutlery. I was about to say that this had nothing to do with me, all this restless arranging of objects, when she walked out the room and disappeared amongst a throng of blackberry bushes. I didn't try to follow her. She was a strong, quick, angry girl and anyway, I was hungry.

§

I met Sarah five days later, at the Mudrazoyle Cafe on Little Chopping Road. We each ordered a hot chocolate. The counter girl only half filled my cup and I wondered if she was acting on instructions to be minimalistic with the water supplies. I voiced my suspicion. Sarah, naturally, shot me a contemptuous look.
"You're an idiot." She laughed.
"Cheers."
"Pleasure. Oh, by the way, have you met my new friend."
"No, I ..."
"I'll get him," she said, reaching for her bag, ripping at the zip, then slowly dropping a giant stuffed woolly mammoth onto the salt encrusted table.
"Well, what d'you think?"
"Yeah, brilliant ... has he or she got a name?"
"I don't want to spoil him."
"No, er, absolutely. Well, he's ... he's a pretty good guard anyway. What made you capture the beast?"
"It was my psychiatrist's idea, actually. She said it would do wonders for my self esteem if I could have someone or something that was completely dependent on me!"
"So ... you got a stuffed woolly mammoth?"
"Appearances, appearances, appearances, so crucial yet so deceptive," tutted Sarah, unbuttoning the skin

on her creature's ribcage to reveal a shining, caterpillar-like carcass of unknown origin.
"This is Cedric, or 'my future' as he should otherwise be known," said Sarah, grandly.
"He looks like he could do with a drink," I replied, trying to work out where the mammoth costume had gone. Although I didn't think the silent toy was a bad idea, after all everybody needs a loyal disciple. I was surprised at the enthusiasm with which Sarah had thrown herself into the concept. Every rifle blazing. She was at the counter now, ordering a flapjack and orangeade so 'Cedric won't feel left out'.
"He's not a fan of hot drinks, then," I murmured on her return.
"Oh, no, they always bring him out in a rash," noted Sarah, grimacing as if to illustrate a point in history when this had happened. Cedric merely smiled. He knew his place in the great dream of things.
"How's Miranda? I haven't seen her at college the last few days," I said, avoiding the caterpillar's glaring eyes.
"Didn't you know? She got a part in the film they're making about Jebbiscon Tundell ... left the course right away. I don't think she wanted anyone at the college to know, especially not any of the governing body, but there was no way she could escape me without an explanation!" boasted Sarah.
"Yeah. Fuck. Isn't the film being sponsored by that foreign company with the soupoholic chairman?"
"Vista Vendetten ... yep, that's the one. They're in partnership with our dear government, hoping to make a few billion when it plays to an American audience. I suppose we, the north sea people, will have to scrap amongst ourselves for the leftovers," continued Sarah cheerfully.
"And is there any plot or storyline to this masterpiece?"
"Oh yes, it's quite breathtaking. What happens is that an old lady called Janimillia runs a roadside cafe for many years while living in a state of constant bitterness at having been refused a job in the fire

service the day after leaving school. Alone in hostile country, bitter and friendless, she devises a revenge plan. She drugs every one of her customers with a strange triangular pill, developed to aid the acute fear of smoke and flames prevalent in the kangaroo population of Australia. It's a long shot. She's hoping this powerful hallindogenic will put so many people off a career in the service (its effects last a lifetime) that staff shortage lists will quadruple and she would get the frontline role she'd always desired. In reality of course her plans are swiftly thwarted. The cafe's chief supplier proves to be entirely unreliable and instead of bringing the correct concoction, he delivers chemical waste which has been left in the rain outside the Kaldergralst laboratory experimental centre. The rest of the film focuses on a randomly plucked selection of customers who unwittingly take these drugs and consequently endure various obscure physical deformities, alongside the inevitable character alteration, and healthy lashings of fear and confusion amongst their friends and love interests."

"Sounds alright. I've seen worse. Where are they doing all the filming?"

"Mostly in the studios ... but also on the edge of a quiet country road in the Piratehill area," said Sarah, softly.

"That's not very far. Maybe we could go and spy on them and see if Miranda really is involved."

"Oh, there's no doubt. I've seen the contract."

"Let me guess; six hundred thousand up front and a triple-pronged yacht with free L.A. apartments to follow?"

"Nearly. Four years' worth of free cheese sandwiches and a West Glamorgan beach hut up front, with obscurity and feelings of worthlessness to follow ..."

"They can't do that, can they? If Miranda really is getting a leading role in the drama then she should be paid accordingly. It's only fair. Stars receive a third of all profits and the rest is used by the state to promote art projects on a local and national level."

"Oh, don't be so immature! It's embarrassing. We all know that Miranda's biggest problem is envy and that she'd do anything to match the wealth and power of whatever other celebs happen to be appearing in the picture. That girl would sooner be an underwater mountain than a hilltop pine tree!"
"So, you think she'll want to leave for the land where the jam never sets?" I asked after a long pause in which Cedric made several half-hearted swipes at the flapjack.
"D-e-r-rr," replied Sarah.
"We could always kidnap her and see how everything pans out?" I suggested, my voice devoid of all conviction.
"A little too much ammunition for the enemy abroad, perhaps?"
"Yeah, they'd love something like that in the Casino Times. 'HELPLESS ACTING STARLET DENIED ENTRY to FREE WORLD FOR FEAR OF HER REVEALING THE TRUTH OF ENGLISH DICTATORSHIP'S LATEST ECONOMIC NIGHTMARE.'"
"They'd never believe we cared," said Sarah.
"Who knows whether they believe in anything, except maybe the concept of healthy grass glowing green."
"Fancy some orangeade?" she asked, exasperated at Cedric's ability to survive on such meagre rations and wondering if she'd ever be able to do the same.

§

I returned to Chokeenaw in a cocoa-induced haze.
I felt awful, though I had plans. Big plans. I went straight out onto the lawn and made a brief attempt at trying to find the lucky copper bracelet I'd left on the grass some five days earlier. Surprisingly enough the ticket soon turned up, although in a slightly different place to where I'd expected, and I was glad to enter the house with a sense of complete security against any evils which may have been lurking therein. The door was slightly ajar. I danced in

without touching the wood, and hung my coat on a vacant hook. Songs of running water serenaded me. Somebody was suffering a distinctly bath-related experience. I assessed the likely candidates, struck them off my list, and mad a dash for the TV viewing quarters. A cruel vision awaited me. Mrs Coddey was wearing a completely unforgettable pair of tight indigo jeans, decorated with tiny, stamp-size, pieces of denim which showed families sitting down for a meal. Her old green cardigan was gone and in its place shone a bright red bingo caller's dinner jacket, the outer layers slashed, fashionably, around the heart area.

"What do you think? Doesn't she look fantastic?" said Paul Gilbert, appearing from the adjoining games room.

"If you say so ... I mean, erm, yeah, terrific ... I didn't known you two were friends," I stammered, disbelieving my eyes as Dan walked into the hallway entombed in a girl's swimming costume, snorkel, underwater tracking device and artificial stetson.

"Hello, Melvin. How did it go with Sarah?" he crooned, winking in the window's direction.

"Yeah, okay, have you been to the seaside?"

"In this weather? Don't be ridiculous. I've been out in the swamp looking for fishkeys."

"What in the universe is a fishkey?"

"An aquatic monkey of course. It's like the theory of evolution but in reverse. Imagine there's a place that everybody has to reach in order for the human race to survive as the planet's dominant force for centuries to come. Then, imagine we've all got there and some of the most intelligent have opted for direct return rather than continuing to function as accessories in the rollercoaster of levelled collapse and messianic rebuilding. Well, that's where fishkeys flourish. They've embraced the first dance but their bodies haven't caught up. Although blessed with fins and scales to help facilitate a marine life, they still look too much like apes. Other sea creatures won't accept them. As a consequence, and because of an

unnaturally large mental capacity, the former government advisers ancestors have elected to live beneath marshy exteriors far from the great sea life motorways."
"Would anybody like a jam sandwich?" asked Steve, always anxious to lend a hand with the catering.
"I'd love one, thanks," answered Don.
"You do know that I've left my husband to his matchbox collection and come to live in Steve's cupboard," said Mrs C.
"I had an inkling," muttered Don.
"Where's that bread, Steve? I can almost taste it," I added, my appetite kicking further revelations into touch.

§

Over the next few months we all got on astonishingly well. Mrs Coddey, slowly shedding her obsessive bossy side, became the lungs, soul and meaning of everything that went on while her son Jerry, a respected rural extrovert, began visiting the house at mealtimes. He couldn't cook. Katherine fell in love with him. Steve, meanwhile, surprised everyone, fishkeys included, by sending his designs to local councils and even winning a South Meyrin architecture competition. His sixty foot tall postbox did wonders arousing the dormant passions of Nopplehouse Borough residents and 'NEWS AT TEN WITH LENNY KLAXON' supporters. He was predictably modest about this success, attributing it purely to the fact that few designers were willing to undertake rural projects without some form of bribery being involved. She thought they were more likely to be feigning corruption in a feeble attempt at avoiding the challenge. It was a divisive issue, one that Sam kept out of. Our resident economist was pre-occupied with his pet giraffe's first day at school and had knitted a special satchel to mark the big occasion. It fitted perfectly. We were all impressed.

As for Katherine, our beacon of hope and responsibility, she continued to study mathematics without enthusiasm for many years, until getting a job in the Halven City Council sea-lion education department. It was a steady career. She was paid six months in advance and the sea-lions, generally, were a patient, friendly, happy breed. When the fishkeys eventually recovered their composure, on the sixteenth day of March 2043, they took control of what had been our home for six years and left us all to make our own way in the world again, using a benevolent bureaucratic arm around these slender young shoulders to smooth the path. Only Don decided to remain. He'd become an honorary fishkey, and, as we watched his noble features fade into the mist that fine, spring, morning, we knew it would be the last time we ever saw him. I never tried. The memories were too sacred for such an unwanted intrusion.

§

After leaving college, me, Paul and Sarah moved into an abandoned bakery near the river. It was a glorious venue. Spacious and serene. Sarah, who loved the thought of an endless flood which would drown her painlessly during breakfast, had carried out the negotiation on our behalf. The whirlwind courtship gave birth to a beautiful affair. We kept to ourselves for a great deal of the time but we made each other laugh when things weren't going well, tried not to spend every early evening in the public bars and always avoided pointless nostalgia when a superior option presented itself. Then the inevitable happened.

§

On bonfire night, as diamond rockets snapped the sky, Sarah willingly absolved herself of the responsibility for being one of Brelleland's few sexual non-combatants. The lucky gentleman in question was Paul, who had a better looking voice and more caring nature than most men around him; quadruplets was the eventual outcome of their nocturnal adventure. When they'd finally pledged their lives to one another and drifted away I felt surprisingly cheerful, almost glowing, in the knowledge that I, amongst all the others, had proved to be absolutely and completely untouchable. A thorn in the tulips. A dry trifle. Slowly, however, this contentment began to wane. I found myself feeling increasingly powerless and stale in my own lack of ambition. Loneliness has many vices and one of them was that I had become dangerously infatuated with a thirteen year old girl at the educational establishment where I was now teaching Geography to varying degrees of success. She reminded me of a younger Naomi. Bouncing, purposeful strides, razor sharp cheekbones and a raucous cynical laugh. I did my best to avoid her. I still had some dignity.

§

The neighbours were all on holiday one evening, it being the week of Citizen's revolution day. I was lying on a dust-covered, oily kitchen rug listening to a play on radio nine, when there came a gentle knock at the open patio door.
"Come in, make yourself at home," I called nervously. Heavy footsteps, either an industrial labourer or a well dressed lady, nudged ever closer until a tall, plain woman wearing a flowery, sky blue dress came in to view. She had a pleasant, if unspectacular, face and the kind of neck which suggested power under duress, yet also carrying the burden of secrets which should have been resolved a long, long time ago.
"Miranda ... it ... it is Miranda?" I said, suddenly losing the storyline.
"You haven't been drinking, have you Melvin?" she replied.

"N ... no ... no, just listening to the play ..."
"What's it about?"
"I don't know. I c-c-can't remember now," I answered, climbing slowly up the oven to my bare feet. Miranda took a step closer, moved away again, and then sat on the most bedraggled of my three wooden chairs.
"I've come to tell you about the job, Melvyn, the position as government researcher for learning and psychological development ..."
"But I haven't applied for any job," I protested, wanting to discuss our shared past but not really knowing how to begin.
"Well, you may not have done, but you've been an active party member for many years now and your contribution is widely appreciated ... the job's all yours if you want it. There's no one else more qualified or with such specialised personal skills."
"Taught to me by you, Miranda," I whispered, as the tears soaked out from beneath her eyelashes.
"Don't talk about those things now ... except to say that I think we both loved her for the wrong reasons. Me especially." said Miranda, turning to go.
"Promise me this isn't all an extension of your acting career?" I yelled at her retreating shadow.
"Come to the Central offices tomorrow and find out," she shouted. The door closed behind her, swinging twice and then, finally, clinging to the latch. There were no further tributes.

4351119R00060

Printed in Great Britain
by Amazon.co.uk, Ltd.,
Marston Gate.